MW01029177

INVITING DANGER

Book 1 in the Dangerous Redemption Christian Suspense Collection

ROBERT GOLUBA

Copyright © 2020 by Robert Goluba

All rights reserved

Published by Evertouch Publishing, an imprint of Evertouch Inc.

Gilbert, Arizona

ISBN 978-1-7330513-2-3 (Print)

This book is a work of fiction. Names, places, characters, and incidents are the product of the author's imagination. Any resemblance to actual events or places or persons, living or dead, is entirely coincidental.

Bible quotations are from the New International Version (NIV).

Copyright © 1973, 1978, 1984 by International Bible Society

Edited by Laurel Garver

Cover Design by Stephen Novak

Sign up for the email newsletter at: https://robertgoluba.com/newsletter/

CONNECT WITH ME

Join My New Release Text List

Text **NEW** to **(844) 465-7100** to receive a text notification of each of my new releases. Nothing else. Ever.

CHAPTER ONE

The thick steel door was more than a barrier between Rey Mendoza and the inmate. It was a canyon separating two worlds with opposing desires. The inmate wanted to deal his illegal contraband without interference from the guards. The correction officers demanded full compliance from the inmates, and had the ability to use force to achieve it.

Rey wanted something different. He was in another world altogether.

The sergeant flashed a hand signal to move outside the cell door. Corrections officer Mendoza moved into position and tightened his utility belt. He could feel the blood pumping harder through his neck with each shriek from the inmate that escaped through the small slit in the door. The echoes off the cement corridor walls each returned a more ominous message than the original howls. The exact words were unintelligible, but the tone was clear. The inmate was irritated with the guards plotting their entry outside his door.

"Mendoza, these guys respect you. You enter first to see if you can calm him down. We'll be right behind you if you need us," Rey's sergeant commanded from the opposite side of the door.

The anxious officer turned his gaze from the door handle back to his sergeant. Rey's face conveyed his thoughts without uttering word.

"Come on, Mendoza. Do your thing with this guy."

Treat the inmate with respect and get compliance in return is what Sarge meant. And Rey alone seemed to have any success with it. Usually. He exhaled and lowered the face shield on his helmet. He returned a quick nod. The door swung open and Rey's worst day as a corrections officer began.

The inmate in his nineteenth year of two consecutive life sentences stopped shouting when he saw only one guard enter. He curled his hands into fists the size of softballs and took three steps toward the lone prison guard. When the guard raised his arms in surrender, he paused. "Mendoza?"

"Let's take a deep breath and talk this through," Rey coaxed.

"Not today, Mendoza. I don't want to hear it. Get out!" he yelled in a gravelly voice.

"Hold on. I want to see if we can do this—"

The inmate's anger was coiled like a snake poised to release venom into a victim. Before Rey could finish his request, the entry door slammed, and he found himself on the concrete floor with a convicted murderer on top of him. Rey heard his arm snap before he felt the pain, but it arrived like a tsunami a moment later.

Rey's training and adrenaline kicked in. To protect himself, he held the inmate in a tight headlock with his uninjured arm. He squeezed tighter as the prisoner tried to wiggle and punch his way out. During their struggle. the inmate and Rey ended up by the door, blocking the other officers, who pushed with all their might to enter. The conjoined men moved several inches every time they pushed. Each thrust caused Rey to loosen his grip a little more.

Rey bit down on his lip until the coppery taste of blood kissed his tongue.

Don't let go for anything. Either they come through the door to help or I pass out from the pain.

Rey fought through the pain shooting bolts of lightning

throughout his body. He secured his choke hold on the man whose eyes turned as red as his face.

The inmate stretched his arms until he slipped his fingers under Rey's collar. He yanked and pulled repeatedly until he was nearly out of Rey's grasp. After a powerful tug, Rey flopped back off the inmate onto the floor away from the door. He covered his neck below the helmet with his non-injured arm to block the blows that were sure to come. Two seconds later, when the anticipated punches didn't arrive, he looked up and saw a half dozen corrections officers on top of the inmate. Rey pushed himself over and lay on his back. As he stared at the ceiling, a black tunnel seemed to close around him. It was his last memory of the incident until he reached the ambulance.

On this, the second anniversary of Rey Mendoza's worst day in the Ruben M. Torres prison facility outside of San Antonio, Texas, he passed through employee security checkpoints with the stabbing pains and wail from the ambulance siren still fresh in his mind. His left arm still ached inches above his elbow whenever it rained — a common sensation after a compound fracture of the humerus.

Over the last two years, Rey often questioned the wisdom of his approach with the inmates. His desire was to help them by improving living conditions and focusing on rehabilitation, but his efforts were unsuccessful. He'd yet to save a single inmate from a return visit to prison.

Rey's choice to treat the inmates with respect and dignity was based on the model he experienced in Europe when he was thirteen. He brought the ideology with him on his first day as a corrections officer and he continued to practice it every shift of his six-year career at the Torres prison. It was getting increasingly difficult to execute. His fellow COs' harassment for being too soft on the inmates was taking a toll. Plus, it seemed as if all former inmates were returning to prison as better criminals months after they were released.

Rey rubbed his throbbing arm as he walked down the corridor humming from rain pelting the metal roof. He passed the bulletin board outside of the CO locker room and stopped. He scurried back to the front of the four by six-foot corkboard. Rey focused his attention on a new sheet of paper affixed below Job Postings.

Several weeks earlier, a CO on the day shift had stopped by Rey's locker to share that a new position was about to open in the main office of Texas Department of Criminal Justice or TDCJ in Austin. Rey's wife Christina made it clear months earlier that she felt it was time for Rey to find a new job. Besides Rey's mounting frustration with work, the growing pile of medical debt drove Christina's desire for him to find a new, better paying job. Ever since that conversation, Rey had been passively looking for a new job, but found nothing. This potential job was different though. The position was for communications manager and Rey spent six years in the Air Force in a communications role before his recent stint as a CO. In addition to offering higher pay, the position was based in a modern office in downtown Austin, not a quarter-century old maximum-security prison for men. It seemed like the perfect answer to their prayers.

Rey pulled out his phone, directed it to the job board, and snapped a picture of the position details. He opened the picture and after a quick review, a half smile emerged.

"This could be it."

CHAPTER TWO

Rey found his position behind a wall of reinforced steel and glass for his three to eleven shift. He scanned the empty corridor and let his mind drift.

Lars Poulsen appeared in his thoughts. Rey met the golden-haired Norwegian while Lars was the Prison Officer at Halden Prison in Norway. Rey and his family lived in Germany during his junior high school years while his father, Rodolfo Mendoza, was on an overseas mission at Ramstein Air Force Base. At the time, Rodolfo was a Tech Sergeant and instructor at the 343rd Training Squadron Security Forces in Lackland AFB. He specialized in planning and operations of all law enforcement activities for the air base, including detention and detainment. Rodolfo Mendoza was on orders to review the Norwegian prison system to better understand the low recidivism rate in Scandinavian countries. After twenty years in the USAF Security Forces, Rodolfo Mendoza was ideally suited for the mission.

It was common for Rodolfo to take his family with him during his missions. Three years earlier, he took his eldest son Carlos to Guam for the summer while they constructed a new detention facility. The year prior to being stationed in Germany, he brought Rey along to a week-long conference at the Fort Sill Oklahoma

Regional Correctional Facility. It was Rey's first tour of an active prison with high security inmates.

Rey noticed the contrast in US and Norwegian facilities and inmate behavior within minutes of starting his tour with Lars. The living arrangements was one of the most shocking variations. In Norway, when inmates were not involved in an organized activity, they spent time in their one-hundred square foot cell that looked more like a university dorm room furnished by Ikea than a prison cell. However, that wasn't the starkest contrast Rey noted. He was amazed with the way Lars interacted with the prisoners. He treated them all with grace and dignity and in return they all appeared to respect and obey him. Rey was no expert in prison guard behavior, but even at age thirteen he understood Lars possessed a unique skill.

Rey shadowed Lars in the Haldon Prison for three weeks, while his father met with prison leaders. He had far more freedom and access to the guards and facilities than he did while visiting facilities in the US. Rey couldn't believe his ears when he learned that one prison in Norway didn't even have walls. It was on an island.

On his last day with Lars, Rey interrupted the sentry with the question that had been growing in his mind the previous twenty days.

"Why do you treat the inmates so differently than the other guards?"

Lars smiled through his trimmed beard, put his hand on Rey's shoulder and replied in his thick Norwegian accent. "Jesus commands us to love everyone. I'm treating them the way I'd want to be treated if I was in their situation. They'll eventually leave prison and I hope and pray that each of them will choose to extend love instead of whatever they did to end up here."

"Is that why all the guards treat the inmates so well?"

Lars shook his head. "No, only a few of them. We are trained to treat the inmates well. It's part of our culture and objective here. It's why we believe most inmates don't reoffend and return to serve another sentence in prison. I go the extra mile because that's what Jesus would want me to do."

Lars returned his gaze to the dozens of inmates working on their vegetable garden in the greenhouse. Rey followed suit and marveled at the colorful garden created by convicts.

"This seems like the perfect prison system for any country. Why don't more people know about what you are doing here?" Rey asked.

The lips of the Norwegian CO turned up for a split second. "Most people don't want to hear about the redemption of people who have committed crimes or successful second chances. Too many are attracted to the punishment aspect. We need more people to tell our story."

It was the last words of wisdom from Lars to touch Rey's ears, but the impact would last much longer. Rey was never the same after Norway.

Back in Germany, Rey observed the passion for detention center reform grow in his father. He watched Rodolfo craft detailed plans to transfer some of the Norwegian tactics to US facilities and reduce recidivism. Rey heard the pitch many times and assumed it would be quickly adopted once they returned to the US.

For the next five years after Rodolfo Mendoza and his family returned to Lackland AFB in Texas, he pitched his ideas and plans to officers from captain to colonel. Not a single officer would support his recommendations. Rodolfo was unable to execute his most ambitious and passion-filled plans of his career and his dream died. A part of Rey also died.

CHAPTER THREE

Rey could still picture the look on his father's face like it was yesterday when he set his presentation deck on fire on the grill in their backyard. He observed the collision of anger and sadness consume his father's eyes. Rey didn't recall seeing any tears, but his heart sank when Rodolfo wiped his eyes with this index finger. His hero was in pain and it stung.

What am I doing wrong with the inmates here? Why can't I help anyone?

Rey shook off the internal questions when two inmates entered the pod near him. Rey watched them stop for a brief animated conversation and then continue to another pod. He leaned back in his chair again.

His thoughts turned to his wife, Christina. Rey hoped she would be excited about a new job opportunity. It would require a move from the San Antonio area to Austin, but the pay would be much better. A way to pay down their mountain of medical debt was a goal they both shared. He thought about the new house he'd buy in Austin, the one they discussed after the kids were asleep and they allowed themselves to dream about the perfect home for their family.

From the intercom an announcement blared: "SORT assemble in A block corridor."

The muscles in Rey's arms and legs tightened when he heard the call. He was a member of the Special Operation Reaction Team or SORT and had minutes to report to his new mission. SORT is responsible for handling the most violet inmates or situations that were out of control. Often both.

Goosebumps ran up his arm as his mind took him back to the cold concrete floor two years earlier. That SORT extraction gone wrong twenty-four months ago had created the physical and mental wounds that Rey still battled. All SORT members were always on high alert. It was worse today for Rey. He had a bad feeling about this extraction. It felt eerily similar to the horrible event two years prior.

Rey was the last team member to arrive in the equipment room to suit up. Once he had on his protective gear, he lined up and waited for the sergeant to bark orders. Rey rocked from one foot to the other. Sweat trickled from inside his helmet and down his sideburns. Rey wiped it off with the back of his gloves.

When he felt an elbow to his ribs, he jumped.

"Hey, Mendoza, you see the job board?" a deep, jolly voice said behind him.

Rey turned his head to see it was Big Teddy, as the other COs had dubbed him. His real name was Keith Jansen, and the overgrown toddler was big enough to block the sun, but he always had a smile on his face.

Rey was six inches shorter than Big Teddy, but what he lacked in height, he made up in girth. His thick calves, thighs and forearms complemented his square jaw. Rey appeared fit even while weighing over two hundred pounds. Despite being shorter than half the other COs, Rey had a sturdy build that served him well.

"Fall in," the sergeant barked before Rey could respond to Big Teddy's question.

The team of eight formed two rows of four as they faced the sergeant.

"This inmate was caught smuggling contraband in the sole of his shoes. He got a hold of some metal. We need to remove him for a complete cell sweep. He knows we're coming, so expect a fight."

Rey pulled up his gloves while all the members adjusted their gear one last time.

"Follow protocol and be safe," the sergeant reminded them.

Rey closed his eyes and said some prayers. One for the inmate about to encounter a force of eight men dedicated to removing him from the cell and another for himself. He prayed to apply only the minimum amount of force needed to do the job and for the safety of himself and everyone else involved in the SORT extraction. Rey was thankful that TDCJ installed a policy of all or none for the SORT team for inmate cell extraction missions after his debacle two years earlier. He wouldn't be entering alone this time.

The sergeant gave the command, and the SORT team moved in unison to A block. They stopped outside a three-inch-thick door with a tiny window and a small opening for food. One team member grasped the door handle and began counting down from three. At one, the team of eight moved into the cell like a river rushing into a narrow canyon. Rey was in the second row and saw the inmate resisting the first two officers. Seconds later, the inmate was on the ground, and Rey's job was to secure his legs. The inmate flailed around on the floor and as Rey got closer, the inmate's heel connected with Rey's shin. Pain shot throughout his lower leg. Rey winced and put his hand on the wall to keep from falling over. Still, the inmate's legs kept waving wildly.

Rey saw the inmate breaking free from the first two officers while the remaining four officers tried to secure his arms and hands. He was attempting to flip over onto his stomach, which would give the inmate more leverage to resist, so Rey let gravity take over. He dropped to the ground and landed on the inmate's legs. A half second later, Rey wrapped his arms around both of his legs at the knee and squeezed. He held on as if his life depended on it. Another SORT member bound the inmate's ankles and then his wrists. The struggle was over. Four officers removed the inmate, and Rey limped out of the cell.

Rey slid down the wall and sat on the floor to take the weight off his shin.

"You okay Mendoza? Is it broke?" Big Teddy asked, worry creasing his brow.

Rey gritted his teeth, "Nah, he just got me in the right spot. The pain is starting to subside."

"You may want to go to the infirmary and have them check it out. Just in case."

"I'm sure it's not broken. Thanks, though."

Rey limped back to his station and then his car after his shift was over. He pulled his left leg into his vehicle to avoid sending any more shooting pains from his aching shin throughout his body. Once the ignition was on, he turned on the wipers to remove the rain from earlier in his shift. He looked through the clean windshield at the west wall of the Rueben Torres facility and shook his head.

"This is crazy. I bet Lars never had a day like this in his entire career."

Rey guided his truck to Highway 90 and rolled down his windows. The cool, humid air rushed over his neck and face. Replays of the incident two hours earlier were swept away by the rushing wind. Rey's attention drifted to the monumental task ahead of him as his headlights cut through the moonless Texas night. He committed to applying for the communications manager position and he intended to get it.

The grand oak tree in the front yard cast a long shadow on his house under the streetlight. Rey pulled into the driveway of the small ranch home and parked his truck behind the single-car garage. Country music blared from the house across the street as Rey limped up the stairs to the back door. The music was almost loud enough to drown out the constant barking of their three dogs. He pulled on the screen door and it fell from the hinges on top of Rey.

He tossed it off the aging wood porch into the patches of weeds and grass below.

"I've got to get some of this stuff fixed," he mumbled.

Instead of washing up and going to bed like usual after a shift, Rey opened his laptop on the kitchen counter. Several minutes later, he found the details for the communications manager position on the TDCJ website. He read the duties and requirements four times before he scrolled down to the apply now button. Rey uploaded the resume that he built for the position weeks earlier and completed the rest of the application. Twenty minutes later, a simple click of the submit button was the last step toward a career transformation.

He thought it would be easier to click the button, but he became a CO six years ago for a reason.

The justification Rey and Christina shared with friends and family was the reduction in his travel with the Air Force to be around for his young, growing family with a sick newborn. Their second child Noah was born at thirty-two weeks gestation, weighing only three pounds nine ounces. His lungs were not fully developed, and he had to spend several weeks in the NICU on a respirator until his lungs were strong enough for him to breathe on his own. Everyone understood the rationale for a son to diverge from the path of his career Air Force father, but it was not the only driver for Rey.

It was Norway. Transferring what Rey experienced in Norway to the US still felt right and a CO position was the tool to do it. He was committed to making a difference as a prison guard just like Lars did.

Rey thought about this dream for a moment. Would this job be different? Would this new position put him on the path he was seeking?

He moved his cursor over the button. Yes, it would be different. He could tell the stories that needed to be told in a communications position. He could do so much more than he was able as corrections officer. Rey said a silent prayer and clicked the mouse to submit his application.

Rey stood and pumped his fist in the air. He knew his life was about to change.

CHAPTER FOUR

The next morning, Christina Mendoza slid out of bed and ran her fingers through her short, wavy black hair. She walked over to the window and stretched.

"Good morning," Rey greeted from their bed.

Christina jumped and turned. "I didn't think you'd be up for a couple more hours."

Rey turned and rested his head on one arm. "I know, I couldn't sleep. That position I told you about last month was posted on the billboard yesterday. I applied when I got home last night."

Christina returned a forced smile, "That's great, hon. I'm going to check on the kids."

Rey dropped his head back into his pillow when Christina left the room.

"What's that all about?" Rey muttered to himself.

An hour later, Rey joined Christina in the kitchen. She sipped dark roast coffee and ate toast with chocolate hazelnut spread. Noah and Maddie enjoyed their cereal in bowls covered with illustrations of princesses and comic heroes. Christina scrolled through her phone and did not look up when Rey entered the kitchen. He put his coffee pod into the single-serve coffee maker and waited for his hot, liquid reward.

Once the kids left the table to return to their Lego-building creation, Rey said to Christina, "I thought you'd be excited about this new position."

Christina raised her eyes above the phone with a surprised look. "I am."

She turned her attention back to her social media feed.

"It didn't seem like it when I told you in the bedroom."

Christina put down her phone and let out a sigh. "I am excited, Rey, but I have so much on my plate right now with Noah. The doctor's office is trying to reschedule his appointment to a day I'm scheduled to sub. We need every penny I can make right now subbing for Miss McKay's class. We only have a few more weeks of school before summer break."

Once Rey's cup was filled, he leaned on the counter near Christina. Rey blew into his coffee and took a small sip, "This new position pays a lot more and I have a good shot. It's in communications so it's similar to what I did in the Air Force."

"I hope you get it. It will be a real help long-term. But right now? We are not going to have enough to cover the credit card this month, so we'll get hit with interest."

"Again?"

"Yeah. Even with your insurance, the co-pays and out of pocket expenses have added up. I had to take the last of the savings to make another payment on Noah's balance at the hospital or they were going to tack on a big fine and turn it over to a collection agency. I just pray we don't have any new medical expenses this month."

Christina turned back to her phone, and Rey went out to the living room with his kids. He tweaked his daughter ponytail and ruffled his son's hair.

Cries of "Dad!" came from both.

Rey cherished spending mornings with his kids. Other than his days off, that was the only time he got to see his kids awake. He missed out on so many trips to the park, skinned knees, and dripping ice cream cones. The kids lived a whole different life every day after he left for work at two o'clock. Additional motivation to get the new job.

Rey checked his laptop every hour while Christina and the kids were at school. After checking for a couple hours, a notification of a new email appeared, and the muscles throughout Rey's body tensed up. It was from the Texas Department of Criminal Justice. Rey's trembling hands guided the mouse over the email icon and clicked it open. The first word was all he needed to see to curl his lips upward: *Congratulations.*

They wanted to schedule a phone interview the following week. Rey replied with his availability and then went into his closet to search for his old suit. The dust on the suit jacket may have been five years old. Rey last wore it to his older brother Carlos's wedding in Las Vegas.

The next afternoon, Rey sat down on the couch next to Christina while she fanned herself with a magazine.

"What's up?" she asked.

"I've got a phone interview for the communications manager position."

"That's great. Finally, some good news."

Something in her tone seemed off to Rey. "So…what's up with you?"

Christina sat up and leaned forward. "I've been thinking. Maybe I should see if I can get on full-time again at school now that Noah and Maddie are both in school all day. We sure could use the extra money to pay off all of our bills."

Now six, Noah had spent more time in the hospital than any child should. Besides his several weeks in the NICU after his premature birth, he had a lung disease called bronchopulmonary dysplasia or BPD. Trips to the ER and overnight stays at the hospital were a regular occurrence until Noah turned two. He fully recovered from the BPD, but it left his lungs in a weak and compromised state. Severe asthma arrived next and trips to urgent care and the doctor's office for breathing treatments became the new normal. Despite Rey's medical benefits as a CO, the out-of-pocket expenses were more than the Mendozas could afford and their mound of medical debt grew.

"Honey, before you look for a new job, let's see what happens with my interview. If I get it, we'll have to move to Austin, so we should wait and see."

Christina bit her lip and nodded. "Okay, I'll wait until you know more about this new opportunity, but if you don't get it, I'm going to see about going back full-time."

Rey nodded, but in his heart, he hoped it wouldn't be necessary.

On the day of the phone interview, Rey woke up an hour before his alarm went off. He had to kill three more hours until his call at ten.

He got dressed and started toward the kitchen to get his first cup of coffee. He stopped as he passed his laptop on the family room coffee table. He flipped the laptop open and reviewed his notes for the position requirements, so they were fresh in his mind. After a thorough review, he went into the kitchen and kissed Christina on the cheek.

"Somebody's in a good mood today."

Rey closed the coffee maker on his bold roast coffee pod. "Yeah, I guess I am. I'm feeling good about the phone interview."

"You'll do great." Christina blew into her coffee and took a tiny sip. "I'm going to run some errands after I drop the kids off at school, so you'll have the whole house to yourself for your call."

"Thanks, hon."

Rey's phone rang at precisely ten o'clock. He waited for the second ring so he didn't seem too eager. Rey was ready for every question, and forty minutes into the call, the interviewer surprised him.

"You've answered all my questions, and since you are a current TDCJ employee, I'd like to schedule a second interview with you in Austin."

"That would be great."

Rey pushed the end call button and jumped up from his couch. He did a quick burst of punches like a boxer trading jabs with an invisible foe.

"Yes!" Rey yelled into the empty house.

A week later, Rey left his house just after six a.m.and traveled north on I-35 to downtown Austin. His suit was stiff from dry cleaner starch, and he had a dozen resumes printed on crisp paper inside his new leather portfolio.

Rey pulled into the parking lot ninety minutes later and positioned his truck in one of the visitor parking spaces. He exhaled and pulled his portfolio onto his lap. Rey closed his eyes and whispered a prayer. He thanked God for granting him this opportunity and asked for wisdom in his answers. Rey peered at the wide brown eyes looking back at him in the rear-view mirror. He saw steely confidence.

"You got this," Rey said as he slid from his truck.

Six hours later, he emerged from the TDCJ office. The revolving door continued to rotate behind Rey after he pushed his way through. He stopped several feet past where the shade transitioned to bright sunlight. He felt a burst of new energy as the warm sun hit his face. It felt great to be able to walk out of a TDCJ facility without multiple security checks. As soon as Rey shut his truck door, he called Christina.

She answered after one ring, "How'd it go?"

"I think I did good. I was ready for every question, and nothing tripped me up."

"You spent a lot of time prepping. I'm not surprised."

Christina's confidence helped comfort Rey.

"HR said they are doing all their interviews the next two weeks and would be making a decision shortly after that."

Christina cleared her throat. "We'll keep praying for good news."

. . .

Life in the Mendoza household resumed a typical routine over the next three weeks. Christina corralled their young son and daughter and occasionally substituted while Rey worked afternoons.

During the first week of summer break for Christina and the kids, Rey finished his lunch and put his plate in the dishwasher before leaving for his shift. He looked at his phone to check his email, but didn't see anything new since he last looked thirty minutes earlier. He put his phone back on the counter, and it rang. It was an Austin area code, so Rey answered after one ring.

"Hello?"

"Is this Rey Mendoza?"

"Yes, this is Rey."

"I'm calling about the communications manager position. I'm sorry—"

CHAPTER FIVE

Rey only heard every third or fourth word from the woman on the other end of the line. He gathered that he was a finalist with another candidate who had previous experience as a communications manager in the Oklahoma prison system. She apologized again and encouraged Rey to apply for future job openings.

Rey didn't even say good-bye when he ended the call. His head dropped and eyes closed tight. Swaying, he grabbed onto the counter with both hands, then he took a deep breath and wobbled over to the kitchen table. Gravity won and Rey dropped into a chair. He planted his ashen face into his hands.

Heat surged from his gut up to his face. Redness filled his cheeks with a mixture of anger and embarrassment.

"I can't go into work today," he muttered to himself. "I'll call in sick."

Rey scrolled through his phone until he found the number to call in sick. As his finger hovered over the call button, thoughts of Christina popped into his head. She was already stressed about all the debt and working hard to fill in the income gaps from Rey's job. They needed every penny they could earn. He hated seeing

Christina so anxious and didn't want to create any more worries for her.

After a deep sigh, Rey trundled off to get ready for work. He stood in front of the bathroom mirror and adjusted his collar. Dark circles underscored the bloodshot eyes in his reflection. Gone was the confident man Rey saw several weeks earlier.

Minutes later, he heard Christina call from the back door, "Rey? Can you help me unload the groceries before you head to work?"

Rey didn't answer, but froze, panicked. How could he tell Christina? Any reaction he was likely to get—supportive sympathy or her litany of worries about the future—seemed about as appealing as entering another SORT extraction by himself. He crept through the hallway and family room to avoid her, slipped out the front door, and sped off to another shift. He blared the radio so he could drown out all thoughts of the missed communications manager opportunity.

Rey avoided most contact with his family and coworkers for the next week. Every time Christina would ask what was wrong, Rey told her he was stressed out at work.

One evening, Rey sat in the family room and flipped through channels on the television after dinner. After he'd changed the channel for the seventh or eighth time, Christina asked, "Are you going to watch something?"

"I don't know. Nothing looks good!" Rey snapped.

"Don't bite my head off because you're stressed at work. I keep asking what's wrong, hoping you'll feel better if you share you worries with me, but you don't tell me anything."

Rey dropped his feet from the coffee table and leaned forward. "I didn't get the job, okay? They gave it to someone else."

Christina's jaw dropped, and her face softened. She left her chair and sat down next to Rey on the couch. "I'm *so* sorry, honey. I know how much you wanted this job so you could suggest your ideas from Norway. I can't believe they didn't choose you."

Rey shook his head and dropped his eyes to the floor. "It

wasn't just that—I was really hoping for the salary increase. Now we have to figure out how to pay off all the bills."

The room was quiet for a full minute.

"I'll talk to the district and see if they have anything full-time. June is a little late to start looking, but I can still try"

Rey stood up and began pacing in front of the TV. "I would prefer—"

"You'd prefer what?" Christina interrupted, a red tint expanding in her cheeks.

"We both agreed that we'll have more job options in Austin. If you get a full-time job here, we won't be able to move up there. I'd prefer it if you waited to see if I can find something in Austin and then you can look for a full-time teaching opportunity up there."

Christina crossed her arms and exhaled. "Okay, but we need two incomes, so it has to be soon."

For the next month, Rey spent mornings entertaining his kids on summer break and plodded his way through work in the afternoon. One day, Christina took the kids to the municipal pool for the only acceptable outdoor activity under the scorching heat in July. Rey puttered around the house and left for work early. He stopped at a gas station on his way to work and attempted to pay at the pump, but it beeped with a message: CARD DECLINED. Had they hit their credit limit again?

"Great, this week keeps getting better."

After prepaying with cash inside, Rey was trotting back to the pump when his phone rang. It was from an Austin area code.

"This is Rey."

"Hi Rey, this is Linda. I'm calling from the human resources office from the Texas Department of Criminal Justice in Austin. We spoke during an interview up here a couple months ago."

"Yes, I remember."

Rey removed the nozzle, selected the grade and began pumping gas.

"I'm calling because the state legislature came back on a

special session called by the governor and finally passed the budget. It included additional funds for TDCJ. Therefore, we just received approval to fill a new position of assistant communications manager that was previously on hold. We couldn't say anything while you were here until we knew the budget was signed."

"Okay."

Linda continued, "Since you were a final candidate for the communications manager position, the HR team agreed that you'd be a perfect fit for this new position and want to reach out to see if you may be interested. What do you think?"

Rey couldn't find his voice. A range of conflicting emotions rose up inside him. Flattered yet also offended. Excited and appalled. He controlled his swirling emotions and replied, "I'm not sure. I wasn't expecting this."

Linda let out a comforting laugh that eased Rey's mind a bit. "I understand. I'm sure you want a few more details on the position before you commit to anything."

Rey replaced the gas pumped and climbed into his truck. He had a thirty-minute drive before he was in the prison parking lot. "Yes, I'd like to learn more about the position."

Linda shared that the assistant communications manager position would report to the new guy from Oklahoma that took the job Rey felt was rightfully his. Plus, the pay would only be five percent more than he was making now versus the twenty-five percent bump the communications manager position would have provided.

"Do you have any more questions, Mr. Mendoza?"

"No, I think that's it. Can I talk to my wife about it and get back to you?"

"No problem. Please let us know in a couple of days so that we can post the position if you decide not to accept our offer."

Rey clicked the end call button and tossed his phone onto the passenger seat. He pulled over into the next parking lot of a fast food restaurant and got out of his truck. He put both hands on top of his tailgate and looked down at the crumbling asphalt as he steadied his breathing.

"Wow. I wasn't expecting that call."

Rey did two laps around his truck and rested on the bumper for a minute. He followed that up with three more laps as he debated the pros and cons of the offer he just received. Rey wiped the sweat off his forehead with the cuff of his shirt and got back behind the wheel. He turned the key and started the engine.

"Could this still provide the break we need?"

CHAPTER SIX

The offer was in the forefront of Rey's mind, but he never mentioned it to anyone that day. But during the drive back home after his shift, he prayed for guidance on the right path to take.

The next morning, Rey holed up with his laptop to do research on the position and acknowledged that the job responsibilities contained everything he wanted when he first applied. Next, Rey began to envision working in an office in Austin from eight to five. He scrolled to the bottom of the job description and saw the pay grade again. He bit his lower lip and shook his head.

Why couldn't I get the position with the bigger boost in pay that would've helped put a dent in our medical debt? I guess a five percent increase will help a little.

Christina walked in and sat on the guest bed. "My mom offered to take the kids this morning. Could we go out to an early lunch before you head to work? It would lift my spirits."

Rey lurched to his feet; he couldn't contain his secret any longer. "I got a call from TDCJ. They offered me another job."

"What? Is it in Austin?"

"Yeah, it's a new position: assistant communications manager."

Christina beamed as she crossed to him. "That's wonderful Rey. I'm so happy for you." She stood on her tiptoes and planted a kiss on his lips.

Rey pulled away. "I'm not sure I'm going to take it."

Christina's smile vanished. Her eyebrows pinched as she narrowed her eyes, "Why not?"

"The pay is just a little bit more than I'm making now so it may not provide much more if we move up to Austin where the cost of living is higher."

"That's okay. I'll get a full-time teaching job once we get settled in Austin."

Rey walked to the window. "I wish you didn't have to work full-time. We talked about how great it would be if you could stay home with the kids while I worked."

"I remember, but now that both kids are in school all day, it's the perfect time to go back full-time and we need the extra income."

"I know," Rey whispered.

"Plus, you said this position would allow you to achieve the goals you had for years to improve inmate rehabilitation. I thought you wanted this position!"

"I do."

"Then I think you should take it."

Rey leaned forward and buried his face in his hands. "I think I need to take a drive and give this some serious thought. Why don't you go have lunch with one of your girlfriends, hon?"

Rey dressed for work and headed in the direction of the prison. As his truck cut through mirage after mirage on the steamy black Texas highway, he thought about what Christina said.

"I was hoping a new job would provide major changes, Lord," he prayed. "What am I going to do? Stay and keep struggling, or uproot my family? What if a move makes our finances worse?"

Before he reached the prison, Rey pulled off the highway into the massive parking lot of Bass Pro Shop. He could lose himself for hours strolling up and down all the aisles of fishing, hunting and camping gear. Rey wanted to escape the barrage of options racing in his mind, so he went inside. Ninety minutes later he left and grabbed lunch near the prison.

After Rey returned to his truck, he pulled out his phone. He needed to make one more important phone call. Rey dialed Captain Maxwell.

He didn't answer so Rey started to leave him a message. During the message, Rey noticed Captain Maxwell was calling so he clicked over.

"Hey, Chap, sorry it's been so long since I last called. How is everything going at Lackland?"

The Air Force Chaplain chuckled. "It's always great to hear from you, Rey."

The two friends spent the next five minutes catching up on their personal and professional lives in the three months since they last spoke.

"I'm sure you didn't call to hear me complain about Linda's cooking," Captain Maxwell said. "What can I do for you?"

"I have a new opportunity within Texas Department of Criminal Justice and I'm torn about the best path for me to take. I've prayed about it for days, but I'm still on the fence and I'd love to get your thoughts on my options. Just like old times."

Rey explained the new job opportunity and his concerns to his mentor.

"What are the most important things to you Rey?"

"My family, financial security, paying down all the debt, and being a faithful Christian?"

"Anything else?"

Rey paused. "I don't think so."

"Those are all great, but safe answers. I believe something else is driving you. Something we discussed several times in one of my pews."

"I know. I can't seem to shake the feeling of failure for not helping improve prisoners' lives more as a CO. I wonder if I'm running to this new position or away from my failure as a CO."

"I'm aware of all the reforms you want to make within the prison environment and to help inmates avoid returning to prison. Will your new position allow you to do that?"

Rey exhaled. "Yeah, it should. I can help share success stories of other reforms and I'll have access to higher level officials, and likely more influence to make suggestions."

"Sounds like the kind of opportunity you've been searching for."

Rey did not respond. Christina had essentially told him the same thing.

"I have another appointment, Rey, so I've gotta run."

"Chap, I can't thank you enough for all your time and sound advice."

"Do you know what you are going to do now?"

"I think so."

The next morning, rays of sun danced on the coffee table as Rey scrolled through rock climbing blogs while he listened to The Three Tenors belt out opera music in the family room. He was lost in the baritone solo when the back door opened and Christina entered.

Rey turned down the music and bounded into the kitchen. He caught Christina leaning against the counter with a new Texas Living magazine.

"I have something to tell you."

Christina looked up from the cover featuring a large antique clock fixed on a whitewashed ship lap wall.

"I plan to accept the position of assistant communications manager."

"Really? Are you sure?"

"Yeah. I want to start a new career and for us to start a new life in Austin. We can start fresh."

Christina leaned over and put her arms around Rey.

"I think we should buy a new house in Austin and I want it to look just like the pictures in all those magazines you read."

Christina smiled and gave Rey a quick kiss. "That would be really nice."

Rey returned a kiss and smiled.

"Now if you'll excuse me, I have an important call to make."

Rey called Linda at the TDCJ office in Austin and shared his decision to accept their offer. She congratulated him and shared the details on his transition from corrections officer to assistant communications manager.

"Welcome aboard, Mr. Mendoza!"

CHAPTER SEVEN

Rey Mendoza graduated from the University of Texas in San Antonio with a degree in public relations. He considered the Air Force like his father and older brother, but Rey wanted to prove himself on his own path. A rapidly growing PR firm in downtown San Antonio hired Rey for an entry-level social media coordinator position. The one o'clock Friday happy hour events and bring your dog to work were nice perks at first, but Rey didn't have a dog or drink much, so it quickly lost its appeal.

Six months later, Rey was on his way to Air Force basic training. After he graduated from tech school, he spent two years at Aviano Air Base in Italy and two years as a public affairs specialist at Joint Base San Antonio- Lackland. After he received a promotion to senior airman, Rey moved thirty-six miles to Joint Base San Antonio- Randolph Air Base northeast of San Antonio, Texas. That's where he met a stunning schoolteacher at an elementary school just outside his base at a community event.

He caught his first sight of Christina adjusting her raven pixie-cut bangs back above her thick rimmed glasses as she stood in the back of her first-grade classroom. At that moment, Rey forgot he was at the school to promote a literacy program partnering the base with the school. He was mesmerized by her plump raspberry-red lips and the way her dark chocolate-brown eyes glistened behind her glasses. Rey guessed the Latina beauty was near his age, 26, and close to his height in her three-inch heels. She radiated confidence and that drew him to her like a moth to a flame.

Rey had a new mission. He had to take her on a date. At the end of the event, Rey convinced her to share her cell number so he could follow up about the literacy program, but she was not as agreeable to a date. Christina said no twice to his requests to go out for dinner. Christina told Rey that she wasn't interested in dating another indecisive guy trying to figure out what he wanted in a relationship. Rey knew exactly what he wanted so that only made him more determined. He continued to ask until she finally agreed to meet him for coffee.

On their second date, Rey took Christina to Austin for a surprise rock climbing adventure at the Barton Creek Greenbelt. He was hoping to show off his above average bouldering skills but was impressed when Christina kept up with him with every foot and hand hold. Rey knew this young lady was special. Within a month, the pair was inseparable, even volunteering together at the center for homeless families of students in Christina's school district.

Rey fell hard for Christina's big heart inside a beautiful shell. Christina would later admit that the clean-shaven man with a high and tight haircut in a military uniform made her weak in her knees. She confessed she was especially attracted to his eyes, describing their light brown color "like coffee with two creamers."

On the anniversary of their first date, Rey and Christina returned to Barton Creek for an afternoon of climbing. Once they reached the top, Rey pulled two unexpected surprises out of his backpack. A set of peanut butter and jelly sandwiches and a diamond ring. Rey received a yes and a no from Christina. She agreed to marry him, but informed Rey that she was allergic to peanuts and would pass on his fine cuisine offering.

Fifteen months after their first date, they married in a small ceremony with close friends and family at a chapel on Lackland Air Base. It was officiated by Rey's friend, the base's chaplain, Captain Maxwell. Five months after their first anniversary, their daughter Maddie turned Christina and Rey into first-time parents.

Two years later, with another child on the way, Rey was facing another overseas deployment. He wasn't sure he wanted that life for his family. Despite his positive memories with Lars in Norway, it hadn't been all roses for Rey during his junior high years in Europe. His overall experience in Germany was negative. For the first time in his life, he was one of only three persons of color in his class. Preteens everywhere can be cruel to anyone they perceive as different. In Germany, Rey and another boy and girl were on the receiving end of racist jokes and physical bullying. That is when Rey found his deep-rooted sense of purpose. He wanted to help and defend people that were overlooked by the masses. He didn't know it yet, but his desire to help the invisible inmates in the US was hatched during these difficult years.

So when Rey was informed that another overseas mission was required if he re-enlisted, he and Christina agreed that he should take his honorable discharge and find a civilian job.

Around the same time, a fellow airman told Rey about an open position for a correctional officer position at Ruben M. Torres Unit. As a member of the military, Rey could get hired without taking the correctional officer pre-employment test. It would be a slight bump in pay over his current Air Force income and keep him home more often to help Christina with the kids.

Rey's father Rodolfo called when he heard the news.

"What's this I hear about you not re-enlisting?"

Rey was expecting the call and the question. His dad was a thirty-year career airman who'd retired four years earlier and relocated to Colorado Springs. In retirement, he continued to teach a course on security and detention at the US Air Force Academy as well as Pikes Peak Community College. He also advised the El Paso County Sheriff's department on their detention operations.

"I know you're disappointed, Papa, but I need to be around for Christina and the kids. Especially now with Noah in the hospital. It's the right move for us."

"I understand. It's just sad that it didn't work out for you. I thought I was able to give my family a good life with my career in the Air Force. At least Carlos seems to be happy now that he's in Guam."

"Papa, you gave us a great life and I'm grateful for everything the Air Force was able to provide me. I just need to be home more often, so that's why I'm going to be a corrections officer."

"Is that the only reason?"

Rey didn't respond.

"Don't dive into the prison system for me, Rey. I'm at peace with everything that happened."

"I'm doing this for my family," Rey said.

It was Rodolfo's turn to be silent.

"Look, Papa, I'm not going to deny that a part of me still wants to see your vision adopted in our prisons. I supported you one-hundred percent when you created your proposal, so that's not just going to go away."

Rodolfo sighed. "I understand, son, but don't repeat the same mistakes I did. It was one of the low points in my career – and my life."

The call ended, but Rodolfo's final words hung like a dense fog in Rey's mind. The look of defeat on his father's face in the flickering light of his burning presentation deck still haunted Rey.

Am I heading for a great opportunity to influence change? Or am I heading toward a brick wall with my foot slammed on the pedal?

Rey wished he knew.

CHAPTER EIGHT

In order to make some additional money before he converted from an hourly to salary position, Rey took on an extra day shift for a co-worker on Saturday.

Despite the seemingly great opportunity in Austin, Rey couldn't shake the feeling that he was running from his failure as a CO. He committed six years of his life to duplicating what Lars did in Norway, but without a single success to show for it.

Rey debated whether or not he was making the right decision during his commute to work, the walk across the parking lot, and through the security checkpoints into the locker room.

This time it has to work out, Rey thought.

Rey ended his mental debate after he attended the daily safety briefing and roll call. "Mendoza" was scribbled next to transfer duty for his shift. Transfer duty required that Rey and his fellow COs ensure all inmates were transferred from their pods or cells to the yard for their outdoor time. Transfer duty also involved escorting inmates to other appointments like attorney meetings, doctor visits, or any other reason an inmate was authorized to leave his cell. It was not as mundane as some other duties, especially because confrontations with inmates were far more likely. It was not something Rey did often during the afternoon shift, so he had to be fully aware and alert this shift.

The first half of his shift was quiet, but it didn't last. Rey received a call on his radio that an inmate required a transfer from the infirmary to the yard.

Rey arrived at the infirmary with another officer to transfer the inmate, who'd had his stitches above his left eye removed after a fistfight in B pod last week. They led the inmate through a maze of corridors with secure doors and cameras. As they waited to hear the buzz with approval to proceed through their last checkpoint, the inmate turned to Rey, saying, "Don't cry, bro."

Rey tilted his head and turned toward the inmate. "What did you say?"

"I know you. The CO counselor. You used to be one of the few guards to smile. You even helped my boy in C pod get a message to his old man before he kicked the bucket. That was cool, but now you've always got a scowl on your face."

Rey felt the adrenaline slam into his gut. What kind of face is he talking about?

"Nothing's changed. Just a lot going on. You need something?"

The inmate shook his head as he shuffled his feet. "You ain't a real CO, man. You're different. You care too much about us for a CO. You shouldn't be working here."

Rey wanted to object, but his words stuck deep in his throat. He looked to the other CO behind the inmate. His expressionless face told Rey he couldn't care less about this conversation.

"That's not—" Rey started, but the door buzzed so the transfer could continue.

The other CO opened the door, and the yard was in view. The inmate took several steps past the door and turned back to Rey.

"This ain't for you. Get out while you can, man."

The other CO replied, "Shut up and get to the yard."

Rey watched the inmate strut into the sunlight, but his parting words hung with him like fog in a cold valley. He couldn't shake the inmate's words the rest of the shift.

During the drive home, he kept the windows up to keep the cool air in and the warm Texas air out. The soothing rhythm of the fan blowing frigid air let Rey's mind drift. He kept running the inmate's words through his head.

Rey jumped in his seat and turned his full attention back to the road after a muscle car passed him on the two-lane highway and pulled back into his lane forty yards ahead of him.

"Whoa!"

Rey looked down at the speedometer and noticed he was driving five miles below the speed limit. He pressed harder on the accelerator, and his engine responded. A maroon SUV appeared in his side mirror as it attempted to pass him. Rey held his breath when a semi-truck emerged over a small hill bearing down on the SUV several feet away from his truck door. He braked to create room for the SUV to quickly pull into his lane. The driver aimed the SUV into Rey's lane seconds before a fiery collision with the semi.

Rey's knuckles were white when he exhaled. That was a crazy close call.

He looked ahead and saw the SUV was still in trouble. Dust shot in the air as the driver pulled through Rey's lane and into the gravel shoulder and then back into Rey's lane. The SUV barely missed two oncoming vehicles when it crossed several feet over the double yellow line on the highway. One final overcorrection sent the SUV into the shallow ditch. Three tons of steel rolled over twice before coming to a halt in the ditch.

Rey pulled over and stopped a hundred feet past the SUV resting on its crumpled roof. He darted back to the SUV. Once he arrived at the driver's side door, he kneeled and peered inside. He saw a woman about his age unbuckling her seat belt. She had several scratches and a large cut below her left eye. Rey reached in through the broken glass and tried to help her.

"I'm okay. Don't worry about me. Is my daughter hurt?"

Rey's stomach dropped at the question. He looked in the back seat and saw a dazed young girl in a car seat right behind her mother. She looked two or three years younger than Maddie. Rey pulled at the door multiple times until he cut through the tall, brown grass and opened it wide enough to squeeze in.

"Hold on to me. You'll drop when I get your seatbelt undone."

The girl looked through her tears and curly brown hair at Rey. She nodded and put her arms around his neck. He unbuckled her seat belt and caught her in his outstretched arms. He backed out of the SUV, and her mother appeared next to Rey. A few steps further from the SUV, Rey slid the girl to her mother's waiting arms. She buried her head in her mother's shoulders and wailed.

"Are you okay?"

"Now that I know she's all right, I am too."

"Thank God you were wearing your seat belts."

The mother did not respond as she lowered her daughter down to the ground.

Rey turned his head back to the SUV at the sound of the crackle and snap noises coming from the SUV. Smoke was billowing from under the hood.

"Let's all move back. The engine is on fire."

The mother and daughter moved back twenty yards with Rey. All three turned to watch the smoke grow thicker inside the car.

"What happened?"

"I'm not sure. My tire slipped off the road and into the shoulder and then—""

The little girl released a high-pitched scream and pulled on her mother's hand toward the car. "We've got to get Paisley."

The mother took a few steps toward the car and put her hand over her mouth.

"Is someone else in the car?" Rey cried, panic oozing from his question.

"Paisley is her pet rabbit. She's in a crate in the back seat."

"Paisley. We've got to get Paisley." The young girl hopped and cried for someone to save her pet rabbit.

The mother surveyed the smoked-filled cabin and bent down to her daughter, saying, "It's too dangerous, honey. We'll get you another rabbit as soon as we get home."

Rey heard the exchange and did his own situation analysis. He saw the flames jump from the dry grass to the front of the vehicle resting on the embankment for support. He figured if he could locate the rabbit within a few seconds, he still had time to save it.

"What color is the crate?"

"What?"

"What color is the rabbit crate?" Rey asked as he was moving toward the SUV.

"It's white, and it was on the seat next to my daughter."

The heat of the flames leaned on Rey like a tired giant. He lowered his head as if running to a helicopter to make himself smaller against the growing fire. Rey arrived at the open back door and searched for the crate. I couldn't see any sign of it. He bent down to look in the back, and he saw a white container resting on the roof of the SUV. After gulping fresh air, Rey leaned in and stretched his arm, but could not reach the crate.

Rey tilted his head to get a better angle when he was knocked to his knees from a deafening blast. He shook his head to chase away the stars in his eyes and noticed the front of the SUV was shooting flames three feet high. The passenger front tire blew.

Rey knew he was down to seconds so he leaned in on his tiptoes and reached out as far as he could until his fingertips caught the edge of the crate. Rey flipped it a few more inches closer to him as flames sprung up next to his waist. The crate was no longer visible when he reached out as far as his fingers could reach. Success! He secured two fingers through the grate in the door. A second later, Rey emerged from the SUV with the crate and lumbered back to the mother and daughter. He set the crate down and bent over coughing.

The little girl dropped to her knees and peered inside the crate. The mother came to Rey's side to check on him. After Rey waved her off, they both turned to the young girl and examined her facial expression for an advanced warning of what she would find. A frown appeared followed by more tears.

"She's not moving."

Rey shuffled over and saw the limp body of a furry black rabbit. He turned his head to cough and then pulled the rabbit out of the crate. He wasn't sure how to feel a pulse, so he attempted a move he'd seen on TV a few times. Rey placed the tips of his fingers on the rabbit's underside and moved them in a steady circular motion to stimulate blood flow. Five seconds later, everyone noticed a kick.

A wide smile appeared on the girl's face, and Rey exhaled.

"She's alive," the girl squealed as she took the ebony bunny and hugged it to her chest.

A sheriff's deputy and paramedic arrived on the scene. They treated the mother and conducted their investigation.

As paramedics checked Rey's oxygen saturation, a deputy questioned him about the accident.

"Thank you for stopping, Mr. Mendoza. You saved their lives. You're lucky you didn't inhale more smoke. We'll call you if we have any more questions."

Rey turned back to his truck and began to ascend the shallow ditch.

"Thank you so much for all your help, especially for helping my daughter." The mother shouted over the paramedic's shoulder.

"I'm just glad I was in a position to help."

Rey threw both hands over his steering wheel and drew in a deep breath. The adrenaline began to leave his body, but the deep satisfaction of helping someone in need stuck with him. It reminded him of the joy he'd experienced helping people in the past, and it was the best feeling he'd had in years.

He'd asked God for guidance, and here was the confirmation.

It was critical for him to help others. Helping was ingrained in his soul and his new job was a real opportunity to improve the lives of many people.

"I hear you, Lord. No more second-guessing this move. No more doubts."

CHAPTER NINE

Monday was his first day back on his regular shift since Rey accepted the new position. Today was the day he would turn in his two-week notice. It was the most pleasant commute of his career. During the drive, he pictured his new office, new house, and his happy family.

When Rey arrived in the CO locker room, he couldn't contain his excitement any longer. He told his fellow COs the news. Unsure of how they'd react, he was braced to defend himself from an onslaught of criticism.

One of the most senior corrections officers approached Rey and stood over him while he dressed. Rey swallowed hard. The white-haired CO laughed and congratulated him with a firm punch on his good arm. A couple of friends put him in a headlock. They threated to lock him up and lose the key to prevent him from leaving. Smiles and laughter wafted from the locker room.

The meeting with Rey's sergeant to submit his two-week notice did not go as well.

"Bailing on us, huh?"

"No sir, I'm staying with TDCJ, but I'm moving up to Austin."

"Into a cushy eight-to-five office job."

Rey returned a half smile.

"It's a communications position?"

"That's what I did in the Air Force. It's the right move for my career."

"Fair enough. I expect you to give one hundred percent for the next two weeks."

"Yes, sir."

The rest of July passed in a blur for the Mendozas.

They searched for their dream home but weren't able to find one that met all their wants and needs. It was either in the wrong location, too expensive, or both. After walking through over fifteen homes, Rey convinced Christina to buy a fixer upper. It took some serious selling by Rey because he wasn't especially handy around the house. Fortunately, the kitchen was already remodeled, but that was it. It needed new floors, fixtures, trim and paint in all the rooms in addition to a total gut job in the two bathrooms.

"How are you going to get all this done while you are working?" Christina asked Rey as they walked down the front porch to get away from the realtor and talk in private.

"I know you love the layout and location, plus I love the price. We can hire somebody once we sell the house in San Antonio, but I'll get things started until then. I'll figure out how to do everything. Look at that porch. It's just like how you described the one you always wanted."

Christina turned toward the porch. She examined it from top to bottom and turned back to Rey with a wide smile. "Let's do it."

Their new ranch style home was nestled deep inside a neighborhood that sprouted up in the sixties. Mature oak trees towered over homes, and grass grew between the cracking sidewalks. The dove-white home featured a slate gray front porch keeping watch over a generous patch of grass in the front yard. Four chairs and a small bistro table filled the perch overlooking the street. Christina said she'd like to add a swinging bench on the front porch like she'd seen in a million movies.

Rey got the fourth bedroom he desired. This was the first step toward creating the man cave he'd longed for. Christina achieved the fenced-in backyard high on her wish list. She committed Rey to fix the swing set for Noah and Maddie and promised herself a comfortable chair to watch them in the shade of their sturdy oak tree.

They moved in the weekend before school started. Once they unpacked all the boxes in the kitchen and kids' rooms, Rey separated his clothes in his new closet. For the first time in his adult life, he didn't have to wear a uniform. Instead, he needed to wear church clothes six days a week now. The TDCJ Austin office required employees to dress in business casual, and Rey wanted to make an excellent first impression. The opportunity to wear dress pants and polo shirts instead of the standard-issue corrections officer uniform was an exciting perk.

After dinner, Rey polished his shoes and pressed his clothes like he was preparing for another Air Force inspection. His first day as assistant communications manager started in thirteen hours, and he wanted everything to be perfect.

The alarm went off at six o'clock sharp, and as Rey trundled off to the shower, the skirmish between the excitement and fear in his stomach escalated into a fierce battle. Eating wasn't an option, so he gulped down coffee as he scrolled through his phone at the kitchen table. He arrived thirty-five minutes early and pulled on the large glass door to enter the high-rise building.

Rey entered the lobby and waited. He noticed the disinterested security guard behind the desk. It couldn't be this easy to enter a government building, could it?

Multiple security checkpoints that each took at least five minutes from the locker room to their post was the standard at his old job. Now he was an elevator button away from reaching the twelfth floor where he would be working.

Rey noticed only a few people had trickled into the lobby and taken the elevator. It dawned on him that he'd arrived too early. He found a stiff plastic chair near a wall and sat down to wait.

Twenty minutes later, cars streamed into the parking lot and lines formed at the bank of elevators. Rey joined one group on the elevator and exited to a waiting area on the twelfth floor with a locked glass door. This time he chose a comfy faux leather chair and flipped through a magazine on an end table until someone came from the other side of the glass doors.

"Rey Mendoza?" a woman inquired.

Rey stood up and shook her extended hand.

"Hi, I'm Linda. We met during your interview. I'll get you set up today."

Rey followed Linda to his cubicle with a monitor, a keyboard, and a mouse. A thick binder and a few glossy pamphlets sat stacked neatly next to the console.

"Let's get your paperwork started, and then I'll introduce you to the rest of the team," Linda said as she motioned for Rey to follow her.

Hours later, Linda had introduced Rey to dozens of people working in cubicles and offices. All the new names and faces caused his head to spin when they arrived back at his cubicle. Linda pointed to the empty office across from Rey. "This is Lamar Taylor's office. He's the new communications manager, and you'll be reporting to him. He's still in the process of moving down here so he went back to Oklahoma over the weekend. He'll be in this afternoon, and the two of you can get to know each other."

Rey stuck his head a few inches into the empty office and nodded.

"Take a look over the training materials on your desk, and I'll come back at noon and show you the cafeteria downstairs. The food is actually pretty good."

After lunch, Rey returned to his cubicle and noticed the light on the office across the aisle beaming into the hallway. He saw someone moving inside so Rey leaned in to introduce himself. The man was removing files from a moving box and placing them in his desk drawers. He put his hand up to stop anyone from entering, "I just got in. I'll meet with you this afternoon. Please come back at two."

Rey straightened up and took a step back. The abrupt reply stole his breath, but he eventually mustered enough oxygen to say, "Okay."

Rey went back to his desk. He studied pictures that Christina texted him of Noah and Maddie on their first day of school.

An important day of firsts for all of us. It's a great day.

Over the next hour, he read half of the pamphlets in his three-ring binder.

"Mendoza!" The voice came from the office across his cubicle. Was that his new boss yelling for him?

Rey tiptoed to the doorway and stuck his head inside.

Lamar Taylor motioned for Rey to come in. Rey sat in a chair across from his boss's desk and watched him highlight rows of words on a piece of paper with an orange highlighter.

He never looked up at Rey until his eyes reached the bottom of the page.

"You're a former CO from Torres down in San Antonio, right?"

Rey's eyes narrowed. "Yes, I was a corrections officer there for six years."

Lamar shuffled another sheet of paper off a more massive stack onto his desk. "Good. I'm from Big Mac in Oklahoma. You familiar with it?"

"No. I'm sorry, I've never heard of it."

Mr. Taylor's head snapped up from his desk. "Really? The Oklahoma State Penitentiary in McAlester. They used to do the prison rodeo on ESPN."

Rey smiled, "Oh yeah, I saw that. I didn't know it was called Big Mac."

Lamar maintained his stone face.

Rey shifted his weight in the chair that grew more uncomfortable by the minute.

"I understand you served as a communications officer in the Air Force?"

"Yes, sir."

"I also understand you applied for this position. Is that correct?"

Rey bristled. His new boss seemed hostile to him the moment he entered his office, and Rey had no clue why. He wanted the current discussion to end soon.

Rey nodded.

Mr. Taylor pushed the piece of paper aside and looked Rey in the eye. "I'm a direct person, so I'm not going to beat around the bush. I'll always say what's on my mind."

Rey cleared his throat and clutched the arm of his chair, but didn't reply.

"I don't think either of us is happy with this situation. You want to be in my seat, and I want a colleague I've known since our time together at Oklahoma State University to be in yours. Human resources didn't give me a choice. They just told me you'd be my new assistant. I told them my preferred candidate works for TDCJ in Huntsville, but you already accepted the position. We are both going to put that behind us and do the best job we can for the state of Texas. Are you up for it?"

Rey clenched his jaw and nodded.

"Great, I have a project for you."

His boss pushed over the stack of papers to the middle of his desk. The stack reached just below the midpoint of the nearby coffee cup.

"I printed out all the press releases from TDCJ from the past two years. I want you to identify which press releases got the most positive reactions and why. You and I will perform surgery on the press releases that generated the responses that will be the new standard for us. Is that something you can do?"

Rey tried to resist the disappointment pulsating throughout his body. He didn't want his new boss to know he felt this task was better suited for an intern than an assistant manager. For a moment, Rey wished he was back in San Antonio.

Instead of conveying disappointment, Rey stood up and smiled. "Sounds great. I'll get started right away."

As he grabbed the massive stack of press releases, Rey caught the stunned look on Lamar's face. Rey understood then that his boss was testing him.

Is he hoping I'll get frustrated and quit?

"Not a chance," Rey whispered to himself as he sat down at his desk. "Not a chance."

CHAPTER TEN

The Ford F-150 truck came to a halt in the driveway. Rey looked in the rearview mirror and observed the growing bags under his eyes. He labored to climb the three stairs and slogged into the house. As soon as he walked in, Rey stopped in his tracks. Dinner was ready. Christina and the kids were waiting for him at the kitchen table.

Rey placed his backpack on the counter and walked over to the table. He gave both kids a kiss on the top of their head and ruffled their hair. When Maddie protested, Rey yanked her out of her chair and began swinging her around like a fighter jet. Maddie put out her arms and squealed with glee.

"How was your first day at school?"

"Good" Maddie replied between giggles.

Noah jumped from his chair. "My turn."

"You want a piece of me?" Rey placed Maddie down and puffed out his chest.

"Yeah," Noah yelled and bolted for the family room.

Steps later, Rey caught up and gently tackled his prey. He rolled Noah on his back and pinned him. "One, two, three, I win. I'm still the champion."

Rey rose his arms in victory, but before he could celebrate, he was blind-sided by a seventy-pound lioness. Rey fell to the rug and Maddie jumped on top of her father. Noah joined in next to his sister.

"You want a piece of me?" Noah and Maddie asked their victim as they jumped up and down.

"No, no. I give up."

The kids continued to jump on Rey, so he grabbed both kids by the waist and pinned them.

Noah started to cough, and Rey immediately popped up. He stood Noah up on his feet.

"Okay, we have to settle down now. We can't get too excited."

Rey knelt and faced Noah. "Take deep, slow breaths. Nice and easy."

Once everyone regained their normal breathing, they sat back down at the table.

Christina smiled after everyone was seated. "So how was work?"

"It was fine. How was your day?"

"I was nervous about their first day at a new school, but it went well. As a reward, I took them to the playground at Little Zilker Park after school. We also walked along Ladybird Lake and played in the big grassy park. We need to get a bike rack so we can take bikes the next time we go. When the kids get a little older, I want to rent a canoe on Bartlett Creek. There's so much to do here. I just love it. It's only been a couple days but I'm so glad we moved here."

Christina stood and moved behind Rey. She put her arms around him and leaned her chin on his head. Rey held her tightly. This was the happiest he'd seen Christina in years. He savored her happiness and fed off it. Rey knew if his first day was any indication of how his new job would be with Lamar, he was in for a long and challenging ride. Instead of letting his boss get him down, Rey committed to getting his new home in order.

. . .

Two months after starting, Rey's greatest fears concerning his new position were coming true. He wanted to look forward to getting up every morning with the prospect of changing lives. Instead, his boss micromanaged him and piled on the busy work. The only thing Rey was changing was highlighter colors on each press release.

Lamar had Rey buried behind his cubicle wall drowning in menial work. He was invisible to everyone else in the office, so he had little chance of moving into a new role.

"I almost miss the SORT team. At least I was helping keep order in the prison," Rey muttered under his breath as he analyzed the growing stack of press releases on his desk.

His negative thoughts were interrupted when Lamar stuck his head inside Rey's cubicle and said, "I need you to go to conference room 7 C for me. I have a personal emergency so I can't make it. A representative from communications needs to be in the meeting. You're the only one here, so you'll have to go."

Rey looked up from his stack of pages with yellow and orange highlights. "Okay."

Lamar turned to leave but stopped. "You're there just to take notes. You don't have to participate in any discussion."

Rey wasn't sure what he'd even say since he knew so little of anything else going on within the walls at TDCJ. Rey smiled and Lamar left for the elevator.

It felt great to leave the cubicle and interact with someone other than Lamar. It was Rey's first meeting in the big conference room since he started. He entered the empty room five minutes early and selected a chair farthest from the door. Minutes later, others entered the room and took their seats. Once the last person took her seat, the TDCJ chief of staff stood and moved to the front of the room.

"I set up this meeting after a discussion with the deputy director of purchasing to introduce the rest of you to a potential new vendor. This isn't just another vendor for food, uniforms, or cleaning services. Today, we are meeting a local startup with a new technology that could revolutionize law enforcement. Please welcome John Nickerson, founder and CEO of Sectronix."

A man in a navy-blue suit with wavy golden-brown locks stood up. He was a couple inches taller than Rey, but looked to be even taller with his lean runner-like build. John Nickerson pushed his glasses back with his index finger and moved closer to the screen with his clicker. He shared a couple of slides on his background and the short history of Sectronix.

"Now that you all know me, I'd like to get to know all of you. Could you all introduce yourselves?"

The introductions started to John's left and went around the room. They shared their name, title, and how long they've been working for TDCJ. As the introductions were working their way toward Rey, he realized everyone else in the meeting was a director or higher in title. Rey's right knee bounced rapidly under the table as his turn to introduce himself got closer. After the deputy director of human resources introduced herself, Rey was next. He wiped his sweaty palms on his dress pants and cleared his throat.

"Hi, I'm Rey Mendoza. I'm the assistant communications manager sitting in for Lamar Taylor who couldn't make it due to a personal emergency. I'm new in this role but I've been with TDCJ for over six years. I was a corrections officer in the Rueben Torres facility before taking this role."

"Thank you, Rey. You may be especially interested in this technology with your background." John interjected as he clicked to the next slide.

A logo appeared on the screen. It looked like some type of hand cuffs straight out of a sci-fi movie. Sure Cuffs was written below the logo in large, bold letters.

"Ladies and gentlemen, Sure Cuffs is the latest technology in prison safety. It's unlike anything you've ever seen before. It's unique because we insert tiny rice-sized transmitter chips just under the inmate's skin in ten key areas of their bodies. They'll be located on each side in their inner knee, thigh, upper hip area, elbow, and in the palm of their hand near their thumbs."

John turned his hand around and ran his other index finger down until he came to the base of his thumb in the palm of his hand. "It's placed right about here."

"This placement is important because these ten chips, when activated, secure the inmate's knees together while bringing their arms and hands in tight next to their body. Think of it as a virtual straitjacket with the inmate standing at attention like a soldier. It immediately immobilizes the inmate, rendering them harmless. It gives your correction officers absolute command over the inmates."

John pulled his hands in and stood like a soldier to simulate how an inmate may look after Sure Cuffs is activated.

Rey was impressed. He looked around the room and saw John had everybody's complete attention.

"It's powered by a quarter-sized device with five years of battery life. It's inserted just below the hip, and the inmates never feel it after the insertion wound heals."

John dove deeper into the technology with charts of Sure Cuffs data from the Hays County Jail just south of Austin.

"I am excited to be here presenting to you because we can be the first state to dramatically improve safety for the staff and inmates within our prison system. If every existing and new inmate was outfitted with Sure Cuffs, it would be a game changer for the entire industry. Thank you."

The TDCJ employees applauded when John finished his presentation. Rey was elated that he was able to attend this meeting. These were the type of topics he'd hoped for when he took the job in Austin.

The chief of staff thanked John for the presentation and said the TDCJ team would review his proposal. He escorted John back to the elevator while discussion on Sure Cuffs began in the conference room.

The opportunity to make every TDCJ facility safer for the staff and inmates was something they were all interested in. Rey sensed Sure Cuffs could be a major benefit for TDCJ, but wasn't sure how. As a former CO, he could envision potential hurdles to executing such an ambitious program. Rey quietly wondered how it would be possible to implant transistors in all the inmates without a violent protest among the prisoners. He didn't dare say anything with all the other TDCJ heavyweights in the room.

When the chief of staff returned from escorting John, he turned to the deputy director of risk management.

"This is your area, Jerry, so you can take it from here."

Jerry was a tall, slender man. What was left of his hair was completely gray, but he moved around the room with a sense of quiet authority. "What do y'all think?" he asked.

Several directors spoke up and shared that they liked the concept of Sure Cuffs.

"How about the rest of you? I'd like to hear from everyone."

Similar to the introductions, the answers started at the opposite end of the table from Rey. He grew anxious as each response pushed him closer to the spotlight. This was his first chance to make himself visible to upper management and it was a topic in which he had some expertise. Rey looked toward Jerry after the human resources director finished with her comments. He nodded for Rey to share his thoughts.

"I think it's an interesting concept. Anything that can help improve the safety of the—"

"I'm sorry to interrupt, but could you introduce yourself again? I'm getting old and I've already forgot your name from ninety minutes ago."

Rey swallowed hard. "Oh, okay. I'm Rey Mendoza. I'm the new assistant communications manager. I'm attending because Lamar Taylor had an emergency. Before I started this role, I was a corrections officer for six years."

"Thanks, Rey. What did you think of Sure Cuffs?"

"It's interesting. I believe anything that can improve the safety for the inmates and officers is well worth exploring."

"Great. Thanks, Rey. Judy, how about you?"

Rey raised his hand before Judy could respond. "I'm sorry, but I do have a couple of concerns."

Jerry tilted his head and nodded slowly. A hint of irritation was evident in his voice, "Okay, what are your concerns?"

"Again, I love the concept of Sure Cuffs and the opportunity to improve inmate conditions, but I see potential for abuse of the technology by inmates and officers as well as legal concerns. The inmates are smart and will find ways to use it to their advantage at the expense of other inmates if everyone incarcerated by TDCJ is embedded with Sure Cuffs."

The purchasing director reclined back in his chair. "I didn't see any evidence of that in the Hays County Jail reports where they've been using Sure Cuffs for months. That's a big assumption to make without any evidence to support it."

Rey thought he should have just let it go. His throat constricted and a response was hard to muster. Rey felt the heat of twenty-two eyeballs staring at him. He cleared his throat, straightened up and replied, "I understand. But we all know county jails aren't the same as state prisons—many of their inmates are in for minor offenses or simply can't afford bail. At the Ruben Torres Unit, where I was a corrections officer for six years up until eight weeks ago however, abuse among prison inmates was very real. I think we will have to plan to constantly update the technology and standard operating procedures for Sure Cuffs to stay ahead of the inmates. It could be a perpetual cat-and-mouse game. As far as legal concerns, I think we can all conjure up the headlines the ACLU could generate with a transmitter inserted into every inmate without their consent."

Rey stopped and looked across the table. He saw a few quick nods.

"That's a valid concern, Rey. You bring a unique vantage point to this opportunity that most of us don't have. Thank you for bringing it up. Is that it?" Jerry asked.

Rey began to open his mouth but stopped. He wanted to tell

them that abuse from corrections officers was also a possibility, but he knew he was pushing his luck.

"No, sir. That's it."

Everyone finished sharing their comments with Jerry. He stood up and walked to the end of the long boardroom table.

"I thank all of you for your comments and concerns. Overall, it sounds like we have some support for Sure Cuffs, so I recommend we do a pilot test in one facility to see exactly how it works and what concerns are valid and which are not."

The meeting ended.

Rey bounced out of the conference room with a quiet smile. He not only got to attend a high-level meeting with several of the directors, but he was excited about the pilot test with Sure Cuffs. He wanted to personally track its progress so he could share the Sure Cuffs story if it was successful. His excitement didn't last more than twenty-four hours.

CHAPTER ELEVEN

The next day, Rey heard Lamar enter his office just after ten. Minutes later, he heard Lamar's baritone voice louder than ever before.

"Mendoza!"

Rey entered the office clutching a print-out of the notes he took at the meeting.

Lamar began talking as soon as he entered. "I heard you attended an interesting meeting yesterday. What did you think of the presentation?"

Rey sat down in the chair across from Lamar's desk.

Did Lamar hear good things about me from some of the directors in the meeting? Was he starting to see I was capable of so much more?

"It was informative. The details of the proposal that was shared are all here in the notes I took for you." Rey set the pages on Lamar's desk, but his boss continued to stare him down. He smiled and continued, "I told them I thought this new technology was a good idea but there were some concerns that I wanted to point out."

"I heard that you were quite vocal during the meeting after I said you just needed to take notes. You don't need to get involved in discussions when you are sitting in for me on meetings. I certainly didn't think you would provide suggestions to directors on topics you have no knowledge or expertise."

Rey rolled his neck and pulled at his collar. He felt like the temperature in the room rose thirty degrees. Two months of bottling up his frustration was nearing a breaking point. Rey wasn't sure he could contain it any longer, but he knew he couldn't give Lamar ammunition to let him go with an angry outburst. Lamar's smirk told Rey all he needed to know about his intentions.

Rey concentrated on his breathing and pushed the growing anger back down. He unclenched his jaw and responded.

"No, I wasn't aware of a gag order going into a meeting and I did have constructive feedback for the directors. I have a lot more experience than you are aware, plus none of them have corrections officer experience. They seemed to value my input."

Lamar did not respond.

"Did someone have a concern or complaint with what I said in the meeting?" Rey asked.

Lamar narrowed his eyebrows and wrinkles formed on his forehead. "No, nobody had any questions, but some did think it was unusual for an assistant manager to share his personal opinions with a group of directors. You need to be careful that you only share facts or respond on topics on which you have some level of expertise."

"Mr. Taylor, I have a lot more to offer if you'd just give me the chance. I can share my ideas with you if you'd like so you'll be aware of it before my next meeting."

Lamar leaned back in his chair and launched into a sinister laugh. "There's not going to be a next meeting. I'll be attending all of the updates going forward."

The words that were on the tip of Rey's tongue were sharp and biting. He knew if they slipped out, it would be grounds for termination. Maintaining his composure was getting harder with each passing second he sat across from Lamar.

"You know what?" Rey stopped himself.

"What?" Lamar asked as he leaned forward and tilted his head. The smirk reappeared.

The extra couple of seconds helped Rey catch himself. He knew he was losing his composure and quickly swallowed the words he previously considered.

"I'm just happy I was able to help out when you couldn't make the last meeting. I appreciate it."

Lamar glared into Rey's eyes. It was like a wolf trying to size up his prey to determine if he should attack or move along. Rey finally broke the silence that engulfed the room.

"I have a report that's due soon so if you don't have anything else, I'll get back to my desk so I can submit it on time."

Rey observed a sense of defeat on Lamar's face. Perhaps it was a missed opportunity for Rey's boss to build a case to get rid of him. Lamar looked down to his desk, grabbed his favorite orange highlighter and started to highlight a sentence on a memo.

"Be sure to get that report in on time."

Rey avoided Lamar the rest of the day. He was thankful it was Friday and Lamar normally left early to go back to Oklahoma.

The TDCJ building shrunk in Rey's rear view mirror as he pulled out of the parking and turned his focus to the upcoming weekend.

Rey needed a break from Lamar more than ever before.

CHAPTER TWELVE

Saturday morning, Rey woke early and walked into the guest bedroom. He scanned the ceiling, walls, and floor. Rey moved to the edge of the carpet and secured a portion of the carpet and padding under his finger. He pulled up and toward him.

"Original hardwood floors. That's what I thought."

Rey pulled on the carpet until half of the caramel colored-oak planks were exposed. He transferred the moving boxes off the remaining carpet and removed the other half. Rey rolled up the carpet and pushed the large cylinder of old polyester fibers to one wall.

Christina entered the doorway to the guest bedroom. She stretched and rubbed her eyes.

"What are you doing up so early?"

Rey looked up to Christina. He wiped sweat off his forehead with the back of his work glove.

"I couldn't sleep."

"You're crazy. It's not even seven."

Rey turned back to a stubborn tack strip. He slid a pry bar under a tack strip and said, "I want to get some of the remodeling done, so I had to get started early."

Christina stood in the doorway and watched Rey work. A minute later she left, and Rey continued to concentrate his efforts on the floor in the guest bedroom.

It was past noon before Rey took a break. He found Christina in the kitchen passing out plates of grilled cheese with sliced apples and purple grapes to Maddie and Noah. Rey pulled out a pouch of turkey, swiss cheese, ketchup and a jar of mayonnaise.

"I got a lot done this morning. I exposed the wood floors and shiplap wall in the guest room. Now, I just need to clean up the mess," Rey shared as he mixed the ketchup and mayo together over the turkey on white bread.

Christina tilted her head, "Are you really mixing ketchup and mayo together on turkey?"

"Yep," Rey returned with a devious grin. "You should be used to it by now. I've been doing it for years."

"I still can't believe you do it."

Rey moved next to Christina and put his index finger on the tip of her nose.

"I told you, it's my version of a sun-dried tomato turkey. I didn't get all the fancy food growing up like you did."

Christina wiped off the drywall dust from her nose. She looked down at her dusty fingers. "Be careful with all that dust. That can't be good for Noah."

"I will."

Rey returned to the guest bedroom with a box of garbage bags. He bagged up all the small pieces of drywall he removed to expose the wooden shiplap wall. Once a bag was nearly full, he double bagged each one before he carried it through the house to the trash in the side yard.

"That should keep the dust to a minimum for Noah," Rey whispered himself as he tightened the ties on a bag full of gypsum drywall pieces.

Christina stuck her head into the room, "Are you going to be ready in an hour? We're going to Nicki and Shawn's house for a cookout and I don't want to be late."

Nicki Pearson was a former teacher and co-worker with Christina back in San Antonio who also moved up to Austin. Christina reconnected with Nicki after they knew Rey was getting a job in Austin.

"Yeah, I just need to get the carpet out and I'll jump in the shower."

Rey brushed off all the small pieces of drywall that fell onto the rolled-up carpet. He calculated that it was quickest to pick up one end of the eight-foot-long roll and carefully drag it through the kitchen to the side yard.

The end of the carpet rested on Rey's shoulder as he turned to leave the guest room and complete his clean up. The long grey tube of carpet looked like a long dinosaur tail behind Rey as he left the guest room.

Rey turned into the hallway at full walk speed when the roll of carpet tumbled off his shoulder. It slammed on the floor sending a plume of dust throughout the hall.

"What's going on?" Christina yelled as she left the master bedroom.

Rey met her in the hallway filled with a white fog of drywall dust.

"Hurry up and shut Noah and Maddie's doors."

Rey leapt over the carpet to close Noah's door. His son, sitting on his bedroom floor playing with two toy F-16 fighter jets, looked up with alarm at Rey yanking his door closed. Maddie's door was closed a few seconds later.

"What happened?" Christina asked as her eyes was fixed on the dust settling throughout the hallway.

"I was trying to hurry, and the other end of the carpet got stuck on a nail, so it fell off my shoulder when I was trying to take it out."

"This dust is horrible for Noah. Maybe we shouldn't be remodeling the house with him in it."

"I think he's okay. I shut the door pretty fast and I didn't see any dust in his room yet."

"I hope so."

"I'll finish cleaning this up and take a quick shower."

The sound of a cough came from Noah's room.

Christina was first through the door and Rey was right behind her. Noah had dropped both fighter jets and reclined back on his elbows. His eyes were wide open and his chest heaved like the wind was knocked out of him. Christina swooped him up and scampered to the front porch. Rey followed and they both watched every expansion and contraction of Noah's tiny chest as he struggled to fill his lungs with oxygen.

"Go get his peak flow meter," Christina barked.

Rey returned with the device that measures lung capacity.

"Honey, we need to test your lungs right now. Try to blow in the tube as hard as you can."

Noah positioned his lips around the mouthpiece and blew into it.

The indicator moved up three quarters to the target.

"We've got to get him to the ER. Go get Maddie and I'll get him in the car," Christina said, already on the move.

At the hospital, Rey held Christina's hand as they both stood next to the bed while the ER nurse checked Noah's vitals and the doctor jotted down notes on her tablet. The rhythmic sound of the heart monitor and ventilator in the background was a familiar, but unwelcome sound to the Mendozas.

The doctor looked up from her tablet and pushed her black bangs back over her ears.

"He's back to full capacity in his lungs now, but I want to keep him overnight for observation. He inhaled a lot of dust."

Christina dropped Rey's hand and moved up to give Noah a kiss on the forehead.

"I'll be here all night for you, honey."

Christina turned to Rey, "Take Maddie back so she can sleep in her own bed tonight."

Rey looked down at his watch, "I will but it's still early. We'll stay here until it's time for bed and then I'll take her home."

After Noah was moved into his own room, Christina, Rey, and Maddie joined him. Maddie played on her tablet and Rey and Christina stared at their son watching TV. Fewer than a dozen words were spoken during the final two hours Rey and Maddie were in the room.

The next morning, Rey received a text that the doctor was releasing Noah at ten. He stopped and got balloons on the way to the hospital to pick up Noah and Christina.

On the ride home, Maddie and Noah bopped each other with balloons in the backseat and giggled. Rey was relieved to hear them having fun.

"Both of you grab some balloons when you head inside." Rey told the kids when they pulled into their driveway.

Christina quickly put up both hands. "No, both of you stay here. I'll come back out for you in a minute. Rey, I'd like to talk to you inside for a minute."

Christina entered first and zipped back to the hallway. Rey caught up a few seconds later.

Christina shook her head. "I can't believe this happened. It could have been so much worse for Noah."

"It was an accident. It will never happen again."

"I know you didn't do it on purpose Rey, but that doesn't make it any safer for Noah. We have months of remodeling to do in this house and I don't think it's safe for Noah or Maddie to be here."

"I'll be more careful. I know how dangerous dust and airborne particles can be to him."

Christina shook her head slowly and was silent for a moment. "It's too dangerous here for Noah. I'm going to take both kids back to our house in San Antonio until the remodel is done."

"What? That seems like a pretty drastic decision because of one accident."

Christina took several steps toward Rey. He saw her eyes filled with tears.

"This isn't a punishment. It's to protect our son. I can't fathom another trip to the ER after all we've been through. Not to mention, we've got another hospital bill to add to our pile. We have to do this."

"Let's just stop all construction, then. We can remodel the house another time." Rey shot back.

Christina grabbed Rey's hand, "Just hurry up and finish it so we can live in the house we want. This won't be easy on any of us. The kids will have to go back to their old schools and we'll be living in two different cities, but we have to do it."

Rey took a step back and leaned against the wall.

"You'll come back as soon as the house is ready?"

"Yes, I'll have my parents watch the kids once in a while and I'll come up and help you."

"Are you sure this is the only way?"

"I can't have our kids living somewhere that I don't feel is safe."

CHAPTER THIRTEEN

Rey finished loading several suitcases and bags full of linens, clothes, and toys into the SUV. Tonight, they'd have to camp on air mattresses. But Christina's parents had put some spare furniture in storage after they downsized, and hopefully their church could supply the rest of what they needed. It sickened him to think of his family living like refugees in that empty house.

Christina hopped into the driver's seat and shut the door.

Rey leaned in the open window. "Are you sure you need to do this?"

Christina nodded. "I need to go as much for my sanity as I do our safety. Just hurry up with the remodel so we can get back here soon."

He leaned in further until he could reach her lips.

"Call me when you get settled at the old house. Love you."

Over the next four months, Rey worked diligently on the home renovations, but he was over matched. He spent more time watching how-to videos and reworking failed attempts to update their home.

At work, he maintained a low profile. Rey questioned nothing he was told to do and left on time each day. Instead of letting his frustration at work fester, Rey focused his energy on getting Christina and the kids back home as soon as possible.

Rey was still excluded from all Sure Cuffs meetings, but he read every communication on the progress of the pilot program since its birth three months earlier. One morning, he was shocked to see a memo calling for an emergency meeting on Sure Cuffs at two o'clock that afternoon.

Rey leaned back in his chair and wished he could be in the meeting. He suspected they ran into more problems he forecasted and hoped that they wouldn't give up on a program that could usher in the type of changes he dreamt about as a CO.

While Rey was editing a new press release, Lamar stepped into his cubicle without warning. Rey jumped at the unexpected sight of his disgruntled supervisor. He knew Lamar was in an emergency meeting and couldn't imagine it ended after only thirty minutes. The look on Lamar's face concerned Rey. He looked like he was in pain.

"Rey, you need to drop what you're doing and come with me right away."

Rey didn't hesitate. He grabbed his notepad and pushed his chair back from his desk. It was the first time Lamar had used his first name.

Lamar turned around and strutted down the hallway. Rey had to jog to catch up. He followed his boss into the conference room and saw an open seat at the far end of the board room table. He tried to remain inconspicuous while he sat down.

Jerry, the deputy director of risk management, immediately acknowledged Rey. "Thank you for coming on such short notice. We had problems related to many of the concerns you had going into this pilot program. I thought you might contribute your unique perspective as we determine the fate of this program."

Rey was still getting his bearings after the abrupt invitation and could only muster a nod of his head. The deputy director continued with his brief and outlined the reasons that the Sure Cuffs pilot program was in jeopardy.

Jerry shared that two corrections officers activated Sure Cuffs without justification to retaliate against multiple inmates. Then he dropped the news of a lawsuit. The ACLU got wind of the program and threatened a lawsuit if TDCJ intended to make embedding Sure Cuffs' transistors mandatory for all inmates.

Jerry walked to the end of the board room table, placed his palms on the smooth cherrywood, and leaned toward the audience. "In light of these facts, I don't see how we can continue with this pilot program. I see too many obstacles, not to mention the threat of a lawsuit that our legal team says would be nearly impossible to defend. Unless somebody has some suggestions that we haven't thought of yet, I move that we terminate be Sure Cuffs pilot program."

Jerry scanned the room. Two hands went up. The deputy directors in finance and purchasing offered their suggestions to keep Sure Cuffs.

"Those are some interesting options to consider, but that still doesn't address the lawsuit that's pending."

Jerry turned his attention to Lamar. He squirmed in his chair and shook his head. "Sorry, I have nothing to add."

Next, Jerry turned to Rey.

"How about you? You forecasted some of these issues months ago, so what do you think now?"

Rey paused to consider his response. He looked across the table at Lamar. His eyes were icy, and his body language was unmistakable. Lamar forbid Rey to say anything.

"I can see many of the suggestions mentioned will help with the retaliation and assaults, but the lawsuit is a unique challenge," Rey squeaked.

Rey looked around the room. He considered sharing his vision for Sure Cuffs but wasn't sure if now was the right time. The mental daggers Lamar lobbed at Rey made it risky to share anything, let alone his unusual plan.

"Okay, Rey, thanks for your comment. Is that all?" Jerry asked.

A burst of courage swelled inside Rey. He knew it was now or never to plead his case, and he was ready. These were the people that could approve and execute his plan to bring aspects of his father's recommendations that he devised in Norway into the Texas prison system.

"No, I have something else. It may seem radical at first, but I think it can overcome the potential for a lawsuit, improve inmate and CO safety, and even save TDCJ money."

"You have my attention now," the deputy director of purchasing chirped.

Rey cleared his throat and turned his chair, so he didn't have to see the scowl on Lamar's face. He closed his eyes and pictured Lars. A faint smile appeared on Rey's lips and then he reopened his eyes.

"What if we made Sure Cuffs optional for the inmates, and in return for agreeing to embed Sure Cuffs, they get to leave prison and live in homes with citizens across Texas? It'd be similar to house arrest, but better. We could establish a method to screen the inmates and only allow those that are most likely to thrive in a supportive environment outside the prison walls. I know the idea is way outside the box, but if it worked, it would transform TDCJ for the better like no other program."

A murmur broke out in the room. Rey could hear conversations and words like *crazy, brilliant, it just may work, and we will get sued to the Moon,* were coming from all over the room.

Lamar gasped and shook his head. "What? That's never going to—"

Jerry put up his hand and interrupted Lamar. "Yes, it sounds crazy, but let's hear him out."

Jerry motioned for everybody to quiet down. Once the audience calmed down, he continued. "Rey, that idea is as radical as you warned us, but I'm afraid it's too far outside of the scope of this pilot program. Can I ask how you even came up with an idea like that?"

All eyes turned to Rey. He cleared his throat and began. "I spent a month at the Haldon Maximum Security Prison in Norway about twenty years ago. My father was investigating the Norwegian prison system for the Air Force Security Forces and I was able to go with him for the summer. In Norway, they focus on inmate rehabilitation and their recidivism rate is less than twenty five percent. I know this isn't Norway, but I thought a lot about potential solutions while I was down at Torres on how we could do a better job rehabilitating our inmates so they wouldn't end up right back in prison. What's our recidivism rate right now? Fifty or sixty percent?"

Several directors looked around until the deputy director of finance replied, "It's a little complicated because so many different things are measured like age, race, number of years after release and state versus federal prisons. However, I believe the Bureau of Justice released a figure north of seventy percent for state prisons within five years of previous release."

Rey took a drink of water. "Thank you. So even with all the programs we offer like school, vocational training, and personal development courses, our rate is nearly triple the rate in Norway. My father also saw the benefits, so he crafted a plan to install some of their procedures in US Military detention centers."

"Where his plans ever used?" Lamar interrupted, likely already knowing the answer. Rey sensed Lamar did not support one bit of his idea. He wasn't sure if it was because Lamar didn't like the concept or because it was his idea. Rey assumed it was the latter.

"No, his plans had some flaws for the time and were never implemented so I used some of his best recommendations as a foundation for my plan. My ideas are focused on providing a better prison environment for rehabilitation since that was a major factor of their success in Norway. Instead of spending all their time around other criminals learning how to become better criminals, I thought we could place them with families that could model positive behavior. They need to learn the type of behavior required to succeed after they serve their sentence, and to be removed from negative influences like those inside the prison walls. In the past, I didn't know how TDCJ could put an inmate with families and make it safe enough for any citizen on the planet to accept it until I saw Sure Cuffs and then it hit me. Sure Cuffs appears to be a viable option to control and subdue inmates, which would make my plan viable to place inmates in residential homes with caring citizen hosts. I know it sounds crazy. However, if it works, the benefits in terms of reduced recidivism and the overall reduction in the prison population would be a game-changer."

The room was silent. Deputy directors shifted in their seats and exchanged glances.

"You've obviously put a lot of thought into your suggestion and it may be just crazy enough to work," the deputy director of finance interjected.

Jerry sat down and looked at all the deputy directors in the room. "I don't know. It sounds interesting, but I don't know how feasible it is. Plus, even if it were possible, I don't know how we would sell it to the senior directors. Let's reconvene in two weeks to discuss a final solution for the Sure Cuffs pilot program."

Jerry turned to Rey as he walked out of the conference room. "Great suggestion, Rey."

CHAPTER FOURTEEN

Rey remained seated while everyone packed their items and departed. He stared at his notes in silence to soak up Jerry's compliment. It felt good to be finally recognized for his ideas.

A minute later, Rey looked up and jerked upright. Lamar was still sitting in complete silence at the other end of the long conference table. He glared at Rey without blinking. Rey couldn't look away and after a short, silent standoff, Lamar stood, shook his head and left the room. Rey imagined he saw steam emitting from his head during the meeting, but he no longer cared. Lamar would never support Rey's desire to provide a better environment for inmates or anything Rey wanted. He needed to take the initiative himself.

It was a Friday afternoon, so after work Rey fired up his truck and turned south on Interstate 35 toward his house in San Antonio. During the drive, Rey played over and over in his head what he said in the meeting. During each replay, his suggestion sounded crazier. His chest tightened and his pulse pounded.

Did I sway anyone in the board room, or do they all think I'm crazy now? What is Lamar going to do to me next week?

Rey pulled onto his old street. He passed the neighbor that

seemed to always have a truck or two in the yard with the hood up and several guys leaning over the engine holding brown bags that hid their large beer cans. Closer to home, he drove by the house with three dogs chained up in the front yard and more plywood than glass for windows. Finally, he dodged a group of kids playing soccer in the street and guided his truck into this driveway behind Christina's SUV.

He looked up and down at the chaotic activity on his street before he entered.

"I won't miss this neighborhood after we sell."

Rey entered his old house and the screen door slammed behind him.

"Daddy!" Both kids ran up to Rey and gave him a hug. Concerns about Lamar and the directors were washed away.

Christina joined the welcoming party a minute later. "How was the drive?"

"The highway is always jammed on a Friday, but not too bad. I'm here now."

"Good." Christina planted a kiss on Rey's cheek and turned back to the kitchen. "Let's catch up in the kitchen while I put the groceries away."

Christina opened the refrigerator and deposited a jar of pickles and a large package of American cheese. "How's work?"

"A little better," Rey said with a weak smile. "Today was definitely better."

"Oh yeah?" Christina stopped putting away groceries and turned toward him. He had her full attention.

"I was invited to the meeting with the directors on the Sure Cuffs pilot program that I told you about before. Remember the one Lamar didn't want me to attend? Today, during the meeting, one of the deputy directors asked Lamar to come get me because he liked the input I provided during the first meeting. They asked for my opinion again and although I could see that Lamar didn't want me to say anything, I gave them my suggestions for the plan I've been working on for years. He was fuming afterwards."

"What were you supposed to do? When directors invite you to a meeting you don't refuse to participate just because your boss doesn't want you to get credit for anything."

Rey smiled at the passion his wife exuded defending him, but he knew his actions would have consequences. "Thanks, honey. I agree, but it can get very political and Lamar is out to get me. I'm certain he'll find a way to retaliate, but I had to do it. It's my only chance of making any of the changes I suggested."

Rey and Christina continued to discuss his day as they finished putting away the groceries. After dinner they drove the kids to a park to play in their puffy winter coats after the winter sun set behind the trees. Rey and Christina sat next to each other on a park bench to watch and listen to their kids play.

A couple minutes later, Christina broke the silence. "I think you did the right thing."

Rey tilted his head and placed the back of his index and middle finger on her forehead. "Are you feeling okay?"

Christina slapped his hand down and Rey tipped sideways in laughter.

"How is the remodel going?"

Rey perked up on the park bench. "It's getting close. I'm working a couple of hours every night after work so you can move back in another month or so. My hope is to be hiding eggs for the kids in the new Austin house this Easter."

Christina put her head on Rey's shoulder. "I miss you, Rey. Miss this. All four of us, together." A minute later, she sighed and turned back toward the kids.

Christina leapt to her feet and scanned the park.

Rey tugged at her sleeve. "What's wrong, hon?"

"I can't see either of the kids!"

She jogged closer to the playground equipment, peering around it tensely.

Rey got up and followed her, relieved when her shoulders relaxed. He reached her side and saw Noah and Maddie running on the other side of the slide. Christina exhaled and leaned into Rey.

"I'm ready to go now."

After Rey returned to Austin, he counted down the days to the meeting that would reveal the final decision on the Sure Cuffs pilot program. Rey received an official invite for the meeting, so there would be no last-minute visits from Lamar this time. He dodged his boss the best he could for the next two weeks. Rey responded quickly to all of Lamar's e-mail requests and made sure he was highlighting a press release every time Lamar walked by his desk.

When the time came for the Sure Cuffs meeting, Rey was in the conference room minutes before anybody else. He chose his usual seat in the far corner and opened his notebook, patiently waiting for the meeting to begin.

Once everyone else took their seats, the chief of staff introduced the deputy executive director of TDCJ to the group. This was the supervisor of Jerry from risk management and one of the highest-ranking officers in TDCJ. Rey wondered if that was a good or bad sign for the fate of Sure Cuffs.

"Jerry, you have the floor," the chief of staff said after the introductions. Jerry moved to the front of the room and used his clicker to project PowerPoint slides on the pull-down screen. Each slide gave a chronological recap of the Sure Cuffs pilot program. After he finished his presentation, he moved to the end of the table.

"Now you are all up to speed on the history and current status of the Sure Cuffs pilot program. We agreed two weeks ago that we'd meet again today to make a final decision on Sure Cuffs. I've been working with many of you individually and then with the deputy executive director and we've devised a new direction to take Sure Cuffs." He opened a new presentation on his laptop and clicked to the first slide.

"Sure Cuffs will transition from a safety program for staff and inmates inside our walls to one that places inmates in the homes of citizens in order to reduce the recidivism rate within the Texas Department of Criminal Justice."

Rey couldn't believe his eyes. His dream was becoming a reality.

He looked around the room and noticed several heads turn toward him. He caught the small nods and quick smiles. They knew this was Rey's idea. He couldn't contain his smile. Rey felt light enough to float out of the room.

"This program will be voluntary for the inmates, so this new direction eliminates the threat of a lawsuit. Of course, will have to develop a rigorous screening program for all citizens that agree to host an inmate in their home. A separate screening protocol will be developed for the inmates to ensure this is a safe, productive, and successful program once our testing is complete."

Jerry paused for a drink from his stainless-steel tumbler. "Due to the sensitive nature of this program, the pilot program will be limited to members of TDCJ staff or other law enforcement employees of the state of Texas. We need to have inmates that are part of the test placed with hosts that have an above-average ability to manage an inmate."

A new slide appeared on the screen with the title Manager – Special Projects. Rey's eyes widened when he saw the grade level. It would be the same level as Lamar's job.

"We need to add resources dedicated to crafting the pilot program, so a new management position has been created to focus on the Sure Cuffs pilot program. Since this program will be more technology dependent, the new position will be in the IT department reporting to Marc Scalise, the deputy director of IT. Human resources is finalizing the job description so we can post it as soon as possible. This is an important position for the organization. Whoever takes on this role will be responsible for building and recording all the standard operating procedures of the Sure Cuffs program including citizen and inmate requirements to participate. Any questions?"

Hearing none, Jerry ended the meeting.

Rey was ecstatic about the new direction of the Sure Cuffs program, but the new position was the icing on the cake. The prospect of reporting to a new supervisor was almost too good to be true.

Several directors reached out to shake Rey's hands on his way out. It was the most elation Rey felt since he met the four men that Lars saved from a life of imprisonment.

He bounced down the hall back to his desk, but before he could make it, he was confronted by Lamar.

"Wipe that smile off your face, Mendoza!"

Rey stopped in his tracks. He couldn't speak.

"You think you're a big shot, don't you? Gonna just waltz into a promotion like it's nothing."

Rey stared back at Lamar and remembered the Romans 12 verse his papa often quoted: do not be overcome by evil, but overcome evil with good.

"I think this situation could get me out of your hair, then you can hire the assistant manager you wanted all along. Everyone wins."

Lamar's nostrils flared. He wasn't going to let go of his anger and hatred so easily. 'You're not qualified and you haven't done anything to warrant a promotion since you've worked for me. So don't expect me to give you a glowing recommendation."

"Duly noted," Rey said, keeping his expression blank.

When Lamar stormed away, Rey stood a little straighter as determination welled inside him. *I'm going to do everything in my power to get that job.*

CHAPTER FIFTEEN

Rey wobbled back to his desk, stunned from the virtual blows Lamar delivered in the hall. Rey remained at his desk the rest of the workday and let the sting wear off. He'd use the restroom on the way out. Once Rey heard Lamar pack up and leave, he did the same.

On the way to the elevators, he heard an unfamiliar voice yell out to him. "Hey, Rey, you got a minute?"

"Sure," Rey said as he walked back toward a broad-shouldered man ten years his senior. He had a perfectly pressed steel blue shirt, wire-rim glasses, and graying black hair.

"Hi, Rey, I'm Marc Scalise. I'm the deputy director of information technology."

Rey returned a firm handshake followed by a genuine smile.

"I want to thank you for your suggestions on the pilot program. As you can see, we're incorporating many of them into this new plan. Jerry said he thought you'd be perfect for the new position."

For a moment, Rey was speechless. He recovered his smile first and then his voice.

"Thank you for taking my ideas into consideration. I believe it will foster positive changes for both the inmates and TDCJ. The position sounds like a good fit for me so you can expect to see my application soon."

"Great. It's going be a lot of work, but it will be rewarding if we can produce a meaningful reduction in the recidivism throughout the state's prison population. I'm excited that technology is going to play a major role in these changes."

Rey liked Mr. Scalise as soon as they shook hands. He could be Rey's new supervisor so the stakes of getting the new position were even higher now.

Rey began the ninety-minute commute to his old home in San Antonio. He wished he didn't have to wait so long to tell Christina the good news. Once he was over halfway there, he called her.

"Get the kids ready. We're going out to celebrate as soon as I get home."

"Why? What's going on?"

"It's a surprise."

"You know I hate surprises."

"Okay, I can't tell you everything but I can tell you that it's good news. I'll see you in forty-five minutes so have the kids ready so we can go out right away."

Rey could picture Christina's smile through the phone. "Okay, I'd better go then. See you soon!"

Christina was waiting with the kids at the top of the steps when Rey pulled in. She ushered the kids down the stairs and into Rey's silver Ford F-150 Crew Cab truck. As soon Christina helped the kids buckle in and fastened her seat belt, she turned towards Rey. "Can you tell us now? Please? What is it?"

Rey backed out of the driveway. "Hold on. I'll tell you when we get to the restaurant."

Christina continued to face Rey and stare at him while he drove. Rey sensed she was looking for a hint in his facial expression. A minute later, her gaze was still fixed on his face.

"What?"

"Seriously?" Christina asked.

"Seriously, what?"

"Seriously, are you going to make me wait until we get to the restaurant? What's next? Will I have to wait until we finish dessert?"

"Patience, grasshopper," Rey said with a smirk.

Christina turned back to view the road. "Can you at least tell me where we're going?"

"To the River Walk."

Christina's lips curved up as she clasped her hands together. "This must really be exciting news."

After they parked and walked along the meandering waterway, they selected a restaurant with views of the water. Lights reflected off the rippling river surface and danced with each passing boat filled with merry tourists and locals. After they ordered and placed food in front of their children, Rey was ready to share the good news.

"First, happy Valentine's Day."

Christina gave Rey a gentle push. "That was last week and we agreed we wouldn't celebrate this year. We need to save every penny we can."

"We've celebrated Valentine's Day every year since we met, so I wasn't going to completely forget about it this year. I do have another reason to celebrate."

Three street tacos later, Rey shared a complete recap of the day's events.

"They basically made the position for me. And it's three grade levels higher than what I am today. I'd be reporting to the deputy director of IT and not Lamar anymore. If I get it, I'll be able to influence the changes I've recommended and make more money to put a dent in our bills. It's everything we've been praying for."

Christina leaned over and planted a kiss.

"Eww, mommy just kissed daddy."

Christina looked at Maddie and said, "I sure did. I love this man."

Rey spent the rest of the weekend in San Antonio enjoying

family time and started on his application when he returned to Austin Sunday evening. The following Wednesday, Rey turned in his application for the new manager of special projects position. Over the next two weeks, he attended multiple interviews with a variety of directors and was waiting for a response.

Dodging Lamar after the previous meeting got easier. He stopped talking to Rey and even excluded him from department meetings. Rey watched the rest of the communications team leave their work areas and assemble for a meeting in the conference room. He wondered what Lamar was plotting against him.

"I better get this new job," he whispered to himself. "There's no returning to my current role anymore." It was manager of special projects or bust for Rey.

The phone rang when Rey returned to his cubicle. He saw it was from HR, so he quickly answered.

"This is Rey."

"Hi, Rey, this is Linda. I'm sorry—"

Rey couldn't believe this was happening to him again. His heart raced and then a flurry of thoughts consumed him. Reporting to Lamar, no raise, mounting medical debt and no influence to implement his plans all flooded his mind within seconds.

"Does next week work for you?"

Next week? Rey hadn't heard a word Linda said after "I'm sorry."

"Excuse me, but could you please repeat that?"

"Sure. I said I'm sorry this process is taking so long, but Deputy Director Scalise would like to meet with you when he returns from his trip next week. Are you available to meet with him next Wednesday or Thursday?"

Color returned to Rey's ashen face.

"Ah, let me check my calendar," Rey said in order to stall and let his heart return to a normal pattern. He counted to ten, then replied, "Yep, I'm wide open."

Rey continued to be a man without a department or supervisor. A ship without a harbor. The following Thursday, Rey stood outside the Deputy Director Scalise's office at exactly two o'clock. When Rey entered the office, he noticed one of the HR managers was also there, seated at a small table in the spacious room.

"Have a seat, Rey," the HR manager said with a straight poker face.

Rey sat and braced himself.

"Rey Mendoza, congratulations. We would like to extend you an offer to be the manager of special projects."

After a deep exhale from Rey, the HR manager smiled and slid across the table a manila folder containing a single printed page.

"Take a minute to look it over and let me know if you have any questions," she said.

It was everything Rey had hoped. He would no longer be reporting to Lamar and he would be receiving a twenty percent pay increase. All of the agony he went through with Lamar seemed worth it now. His personal and professional life would be better because of this new position.

Rey looked up from the paper and smiled. "Where do I sign?"

CHAPTER SIXTEEN

Rey quietly packed up his desk in communications after Lamar left early Friday, and started his new position on the fifteenth floor the following Monday. His first major task was writing the first draft of the standard operating procedures for the Sure Cuffs program. He was joined by two additional part-time team members and Sure Cuffs founder John Nickerson. They scheduled their first joint meeting later that week. They had already outlined several pages when Deputy Director Scalise joined them.

Mr. Scalise sat next to Rey. He scanned several documents in front of him and asked, "What are we going to call this program? We need to give it a good name so we can start promoting this internally and then eventually to citizens. Got any ideas?"

Nobody offered any suggestions.

"I kind of like the Sure Cuffs Safety Program," the owner of Sure Cuffs offered.

"John, your Sure Cuffs technology will be part of it, but this program is more than Sure Cuffs. Any other ideas?"

Rey gazed toward the far corner where the wall touched the ceiling as if it contained a vault of brilliant ideas. Seconds later he shook his head. "I don't know, but let me sleep on it and I'll have some suggestions by tomorrow."

Mr. Scalise nodded. "Okay, I think we should all come up with some suggestions to review and then we can make a final decision tomorrow."

That night, Rey couldn't stop thinking about new names for the pilot program.

"SORT was a good name for special operations response team. It explained exactly what it does and was easy to say. The government sure does like its acronyms." Rey said aloud as he sat on the couch and stared at the dark TV.

"Maybe it could be T-CHIP. Texas Citizens Housing Inmates Program." Rey sat up straight as he tossed the name around in his head. "It has a nice ring, but I'm not sure it's clear or attractive."

A minute later, Rey fell back into the plush couch cushions. "No, that's not it."

Rey stood and paced in the family room. "Reduce recidivism, residential house arrest, rehabilitation, return to productive citizenship. It needs something like that in the name to give it some clarity and punch."

Fifteen minutes later Rey threw up his arms. "I've got nothing."

He decided to go to bed in hopes that he could think more clearly in the morning. He desperately wanted to come up with a great name before his meeting tomorrow.

As Rey lay in bed, he tried to think of a name one last time. After midnight, the right name still eluded him, but exhaustion caught up and Rey fell asleep.

He jerked awake sometime later with the perfect name. He fumbled for some paper to jot it down, and realized it was over an hour before his alarm was set to go off. Though he tried to fall back to sleep, excitement won out, so he got up and left for work early. He couldn't wait to share his suggestion.

Not long after the meeting started, Marc Scalise stood up next to the whiteboard.

"So what name did y'all come up with for the pilot program that we can share with the public?"

Carrie, one of the IT project specialists assigned to this team offered some solid suggestions that had the group nodding and pondering, while a guy from desktop services offered a name that missed the mark to a degree that a few in the room laughed.

Mr. Scalise quickly shut down his campaign for his name and turned to Rey. "How about you?"

Rey shuffled through a few pages of notes until he found the one he was looking for.

"Since the program is about rehabilitating inmates and housing them with citizens, I thought it should include those terms in the name. My suggestion is to call it RIHARP, which stands for residential inmate housing and rehabilitation program. Therefore, the story we share with the public is that RIHARP places individuals incarcerated within the Texas criminal justice system into residential homes to provide those inmates a positive environment for optimal rehabilitation prior to their release."

Rey looked to the small team of three and tried to gauge the reaction based on the blank looks on their faces.

After a few uncomfortable seconds of silence, Rey asked, "so what do you think?"

Deputy Director Scalise nodded. "It's growing on me. It's not too bad."

Nobody else spoke, so Mr. Scalise jumped in again. "What does everyone else think?"

Carrie spoke first. "It's pretty good and says what it is. I like it."

The desktop services guy seemed pained to admit defeat, but was able to utter, "it's good."

Mr. Scalise used his fist as a gavel and tapped the table. "RIHARP it is."

Rey was elated. He always thought he had good ideas to contribute but was never given the opportunity to share them, especially with Lamar as his supervisor. For the first time in his adult life, he was given the opportunity to contribute his suggestions and he was taking full advantage of it.

"Last, we need a project name."

All eyes turned to Rey. He shrugged. "My tank is empty after RIHARP."

The room was quiet. Team members took turns looking out the window, at the ceiling and at the conference room table for inspiration.

A minute later, Carrie shrieked, "I've got it! Second Chance. Let's call it Project Second Chance since that's what RIHARP is about. The RIHARP inmates are getting a second chance to turn their lives around."

Glances were exchanged and soon smiles followed. Project Second Chance was quickly approved as the official project name.

For the rest of the day, Rey continued to work with the team on the fine details of Project Second Chance. He was so engrossed that he didn't realize five o'clock had passed forty minutes earlier and most of the office had already departed for home. Rey quickly packed up everything and left the office.

He strutted to his car, satisfied that he was on the right track to lead a new program that will deliver the reforms his father inspired in him. He tapped on his steering wheel like a drum solo and began his trek home.

A few blocks from his house, his cell phone rang on the seat beside him. He checked the caller ID.

"Hi, Mama."

He had to pull over to the side of the road as soon as he heard her speak. She was sobbing loudly into the phone.

"What's wrong?"

"Papa is in surgery. He passed out during training at the community college and the ambulance brought him to the hospital. The doctor thinks he had a heart attack, so they rushed him to surgery a few minutes ago."

"Where are you?"

"We are at, um, it's Saint Frances Medical Center."

"Okay, I'll be there as fast as I can."

"You don't have to rush up here."

"Yes, I do."

When Rey arrived home, he packed a few days' clothes and some snacks. Once he was on the highway headed north, he called Christina.

"I'm heading to Colorado. Papa had a heart attack."

"Oh, my gosh, is he okay?" Christina asked.

"He's in surgery now so we'll know more when he gets out."

"Are you heading to the airport now?"

"I'm not flying. I'm driving."

"That's a long drive. Why don't you fly?"

"It's only twelve or thirteen hours. It costs an arm and leg to fly last minute. I can get there by sunup tomorrow if I drive."

"I don't like the idea of you driving all night. Promise me you'll stop and rest if you get tired. We don't want two people in the hospital."

"I'll be safe and I'll text you when I get there."

Rey hung up and put Colorado Springs into the GPS. It said he would arrive at seven thirty tomorrow morning without stops. Rey managed to keep his few pit stops brief so that he could make it there by eight o'clock.

Rey arrived at Saint Frances Medical Center and was guided to his father's room. He slowed down before he entered. Rey poked his head into the room and saw his mom sitting next to a pale man hooked up to a bunch of machines.

That can't be Papa.

CHAPTER SEVENTEEN

Rey's mother Maria got up to greet her son. They exchanged hugs and moved next to Rodolfo.

"How is he?" Rey asked in a whisper.

"The doctor said the surgery was a success. He had a mild heart attack and they inserted two stents. They said he should make a full recovery."

It was good news, but seeing his hero lying in a hospital bed was hard for Rey. He never knew is father to be anything but a strong and dependable man. Rey pulled a chair over between his mother and father.

For the next hour, Rey watched his father sleep and occasionally dozed off himself. Having been awake for over twenty-four hours straight, he was struggling to keep his heavy eyelids from closing. His mother noticed.

"Rey, you need to get some rest."

"I'm good. I want to see him when he wakes up."

"Honey, he may sleep for a few more hours. They gave him pain medicine after the surgery, and they said he may sleep a while."

Rey looked at his father. The man with salt and pepper hair looked peaceful in his sleep.

"Okay. Just for a minute, though."

Rey slid down in his chair and leaned back until the wall supported his head. Three hours later, he woke to a conversation in the room. He straightened up and saw his mother and father talking.

Rey jumped from his seat and moved to the side of the bed, and asked "How are you feeling?"

Rodolfo swallowed hard and answered in a raspy voice, "Good, all things considered."

"Do you need anything?"

"A drink of water would be nice."

Rey found a glass of water and took it to his father.

"What happened yesterday?"

Rodolfo explained that he felt fine and then after demonstrating a safe detention technique that he'd done hundreds of times, he started to feel lightheaded. A minute later, he was on the concrete floor with the paramedics asking for his name. "I guess I had some blocked arteries, but they fixed them."

"Papa, you need to find a new doctor if they missed blocked arteries. Don't they test for stuff like that after you turn sixty?"

Rodolfo cracked a half smile, but did not respond.

"When was the last time you've seen your doctor?"

Rodolfo took another drink of water. "I've been busy. I'll be better about making my appointments now."

Rey raised his voice, "Grandpa died from a heart attack before he was seventy. Papa, you have to—"

Maria put her hand on Rey's arm. "Not now, Rey. He'll be better in the future. I'll make sure of it. Let him rest now."

He turned to his mother. "I know, but heart disease runs in the family. This was a big scare for all of us."

"He knows."

Rey and his mother found their seats as Rodolfo closed his eyes again.

Maria leaned over to Rey. "Go get something to eat. I'll wait here with him until you get back. The food is pretty good."

Rey didn't even realize how hungry he was until his mother suggested that he eat. He found the cafeteria and devoured a full plate of scrambled eggs with hot sauce and sausage. Rodolfo was sitting up when Rey returned. The color was back in his face.

"Mama, you can go now. I'll hang out with Papa while you eat."

Maria bent over and kissed Rodolfo. A minute later she left the room.

"Thanks for coming, Rey. I know you had to come a long way, but I appreciate you being here. When do you have to get back to work?"

"I took two days of personal time, so I'll head back tomorrow if you're doing okay."

"I'll be fine. How's work going?"

A smile emerged on Rey's face. He pulled his chair closer to the bed.

"It's going great. You're never going to believe what we are doing."

Rey told his father about all the details of RIHARP. He walked around the room and explained how each meeting helped RIHARP morph into a program with components of Rodolfo's plan two decades earlier.

"You were my inspiration for RIHARP," Rey shared with his father.

"That's amazing. I never thought I'd see that day when inmates in the US were treated similar to what we saw in Norway."

The two men ended their conversation when Maria entered with her phone in her hand and her arm extended. "It's Carlos, he wants to talk to you."

Maria, Rodolfo, and Rey spent the rest of the day catching up. Rey filled them in on all the latest news on Noah and Maddie but failed to mention they were living in a different city. He would tell them another time. Today they had enough worries.

The next morning, Rey got breakfast in the hospital cafeteria and packed his gym bag in the hospital room.

"I was hoping I could help walk you to your truck when they discharge you today, but I have a long drive, so I need to head out now," Rey said as he zipped up his bag.

He walked over the bed where his father was sitting up. He looked like his old self again and this reassured Rey it was okay to leave. He leaned over and gave his father a hug.

"Go see your doctor soon and do what he tells you to do."

"I will. Thanks again for driving all the way up here."

"No problem. I'm just glad you are okay. I'm going to be praying for you," Rey said as he shouldered his bag, then gave his mother a hug. "I'll text you when I get back to Austin."

He was nearly out the door when his father called, "Hey, Rey?"

He took a step back into the room.

"I'm proud of you," Papa said.

CHAPTER EIGHTEEN

The thirteen-hour drive back to Austin didn't seem as long as the trip to Colorado Springs. Rey kept playing his father's last words in his mind. It was like music to his ears. It wasn't the first time Rey's father told him he was proud of him, but it always provided fuel for Rey to do more. This time was no exception. In fact, it meant more to Rey because he was pursuing a joint mission with his father. Rodolfo Mendoza was just as responsible for RIHARP as Rey and the success of the program was critical to realizing their shared dream.

Rey returned to work the following day with a fresh perspective. He brought energy to the Project Second Chance team as they marched ahead with the laborious job of creating a brand-new program for TDCJ. While RIHARP was on the right track, Rey still struggled with the physical distance between him and his family. He tried to complete projects around the house but would get discouraged by his lack of construction knowledge and spent hours watching YouTube videos, mostly of home repair tips, but also of fishing and rock climbing when he got too tired to hammer, saw, sand, or paint. He was making progress, but it wasn't fast enough to bring his family home any time soon.

After work one afternoon, Rey pondered his meeting from

earlier that day during his drive home. *What else are we missing to ensure RIHARP is a success?*

When Rey was a few houses away from home, he noticed an officer was sitting on his front steps in a familiar Air Force uniform. Rey wasn't expecting anyone, so he slowed down to get a better look. He stopped in front of his house and the man in the Air Force uniform looked up and locked eyes with Rey. His jaw dropped when he recognized who was sitting on his front porch. Captain Maxwell?

Rey put the vehicle in park and leapt from his truck. The man was already in the driveway when Rey shut his door. They met behind the tailgate of the Ford truck. Rey extended his hand to shake but the six-foot four-inch mountain of a man wasn't interested in a handshake. He spread his arms and gave Rey a firm hug with lots of back slaps.

Captain Maxwell was the Wing Chaplain with Joint Base San Antonio or JBSA. He served as chaplain on both the larger Joint Base San Antonio- Lackland Air Base and the smaller Joint Base San Antonio- Randolph Air Force Base. Rey first met him on JBSA- Lackland when he attended a service at the Freedom Chapel.

Rey credited Captain Maxwell's ministry, especially his sermons, for his deeper connection with Jesus. During Rey's last two years in the Air Force, he started attending services at Randolph's Religious Activity Center, but didn't feel the same connection he did with Captain Maxwell. Six months later, Rey began driving thirty-six miles to Lackland's Freedom Chapel on most Sundays to listen to Captain Maxwell, and continued to do so for the remaining eighteen months he was enlisted.

During that time, Captain Maxwell became a friend and a mentor to Airman Mendoza. Rey confided to Captain Maxwell his drive to make a difference with people that need a second chance. He shared his experience in Norway, his father's plan for reforms and Rey's deep desire to see those plans succeed in the USA. Captain Maxwell was one of the few people supportive of Rey taking the CO position because he understood his aspirations to do more for inmates.

"Hey Chap, it's great to see you. I didn't know you were planning to stop by, or I would have left work earlier."

"Ah, no worries, Rey. I was up in Austin with a delegation at the governor's office. I thought I would drop by on my way home since I hadn't visited since you moved to Austin."

"I'm so glad you did. It's great to see you. Come on in."

The two men entered the quiet house.

"Where's Christina and the kids?"

"Umm. They are down in San Antonio visiting her parents."

Rey convinced himself that it was only a partial lie. He didn't want to tell his friend that his family moved out. At least not right now.

"Oh, that's too bad. I was hoping to see Christina and how much your kiddos have grown."

"She's going to be disappointed that she missed you too. Both kids have shot up since we've last seen you. We'll all have to come visit you at Lackland sometime soon."

Ray grabbed two sodas and led Captain Maxwell into the family room. They both took their seats and sipped their bubbly beverages.

The Air Force Captain spoke first. "How are you liking Austin and the new job?"

Ray smiled and straightened up on the couch. "I'm really loving it now. It was rocky the first six months because my supervisor didn't want me there and did all he could to make my job unbearable. However, I just got a new promotion a couple weeks ago and I love everything about it."

Captain Maxwell responded with his warm, genuine smile. It instantly took Ray back to all the discussions they had inside the Lackland chapel. Captain Maxwell had a way of making Ray feel more valued than ever before and believing that anything he wanted to accomplish was possible. He respected Captain Maxwell as much as anyone.

"That's great, Ray, what's this new position?"

"I'm a manager of special projects. My focus is on a new program TDCJ is going to launch to the public soon. It's very exciting. This program is going to do a lot of good for TDCJ, the inmates and the community."

Captain Maxwell nodded and pursed his lips. "Can you tell me more or is it classified?"

"No, it's not classified. It's a relaunch of a program we announced to the public earlier this year." Rey took a drink and leaned forward. "We'll be outfitting qualified inmates that want to serve their sentence in the homes of Texas citizens. This new technology will allow citizens to subdue them in the event they feel they are in danger. The overall objective of the program is to put inmates in a positive environment with a higher likelihood of rehabilitation, so fewer reoffend after they are released into the public after serving their sentence. Our hope is to release productive members of the community and not better criminals. The opportunity to incorporate some of the things I learned in Norway and improve the lives of inmates and their families has me pretty excited."

"That's amazing, Rey. This sound a lot like the type of thing you been wanting to do for a long time. I think you may have finally found the perfect job for you."

A bright smile engulphed Rey's face. "I think you're right. I feel good every day going to the office knowing that we're going to make a real difference in the lives of people all across Texas."

Rey took another drink from his glass and leaned back into the deep sofa cushions.

"Enough about me, what about you? How's everything at JBSA? How are Linda and the kids?"

The two old friends talked for another hour. Captain Maxwell looked at his watch and said, "I better get going. I was in Guam last week, so I don't want to get home too late tonight. I saw your brother Carlos, by the way. He was pretty shaken by your dad's heart attack, but is doing well otherwise."

Rey nodded. "That's good to hear. I've been calling Papa almost every day to check on him. He can be so stubborn about his health, but between Mama, Carlos, and me he has plenty of encouragement to get better."

Captain Maxwell nodded as he stood.

Rey also got to his feet. "I'm so glad you stopped by. Let's do this again."

Captain Maxwell started toward the door and stopped. "I'm happy for you. You've come a long way and you're in a good spot right now. I'll be praying for you and your family."

Rey went to bed early. He was pleased to spend time with a close friend and for the progress he was making at work, but he felt empty. He lied to a friend and mentor because he knew Captain Maxwell would urge Rey to do everything in his power to get his family back. Christina, Maddie, and Noah were ninety miles away, but it felt like an ocean between them every time he wanted to share his life with the people he loved most.

Rey had to get these house projects done soon. Living apart was getting more painful each passing day.

CHAPTER NINETEEN

Christina leaned over and kissed her dad on the cheek and hugged her mom. "Thanks for lunch. I want to take advantage of how close you are before I move back to Austin."

After lunch with her parents, Christina went clothes shopping for the kids and grabbed a half a cart of groceries before she picked up Maddie and Noah from school.

As soon as Christina stopped in the driveway, the kids unbuckled their seatbelts and began to race inside, a new game they started after they moved back to San Antonio.

As Noah reached the top step, Christina noticed the back door was ajar.

"Stop!" she shouted.

Both kids froze at the volume and tone that were uncommon from their mother. Christina was ninety-nine percent sure she shut and locked the back door when she left—a necessity in their neighborhood. No, she was one hundred percent sure she locked the back door.

"Hurry, come back down here by me."

They both turned and scrambled back to their mother.

Christina moved both children behind her. "Stay by the car until I tell you to move."

Maddie started to cry, but Christina ignored her. She was laser-focused on the back door open several inches. Christina climbed each step with the silence of a lioness. She was listening for a sign of what may be waiting for her behind the door. She turned back to her kids and motioned for them to move farther away.

Christina drew in a deep breath and pushed open the door. As soon as the door was in motion, she backed up to let whatever might be trapped inside escape to safety. Nobody emerged, but a stench did— body odor and stale alcohol. Goosebumps formed on the back of her arms. Her intuition was right. Somebody was inside the house.

Were they still there, or did they leave the door open after they left? Should I call the police now, or should I see if somebody is still there?

A dozen scenarios flooded her mind, but her gut told her to keep going, and so far, it hadn't let her down. Once Christina passed the door jamb, she could pinpoint the source of the smell. A man was sleeping on the kitchen floor. His clothes were soiled and his long beard unkempt.

Christina took a few steps forward. The odor grew stronger with each step. She leaned forward to see if the man was breathing. Christina leaned so far that she lost her balance and bumped a kitchen chair. It screeched across the tile floor, and the man began to stir. He lifted his head and looked around, blinking. A confused expression took over his mud-stained face.

He shook his head and scanned the room again, this time locking eyes with Christina. A scowl formed, and he used the kitchen table to pull himself up. Christina backed up to the open door and watched the man steady himself.

Once he found his sea legs, he glared at Christina. His eyes narrowed. "Get out of here!" the man shouted in a strangled voice. His hollow, pale eyes glared at her.

Those eyes took her back twenty-five years to when Christina was eight. A man with disheveled hair approached Christina and her mom in a parking lot outside a big box store late one night. Christina was able to smell a cocktail of body odor and alcohol from the other side of the car. Most of all, Christina remembered his eyes. The confused, yet haunting look in his dark green eyes just before he attacked was etched deep in her memory. He asked Christina's mom for money, and when she opened her purse, he attacked her. Her mom screamed when she fell back into the driver's seat through the open door. Christina froze while her mom fought the man off until two other men ran over to help. They pulled off the attacker and held him until the police arrived. Christina cried with her mom for ten minutes until the officer tapped on the window. That night, she wept until she ran out of tears. Christina never felt such an intense fear for her family or herself. She vowed to never feel like that again.

"Get out of my house right now," the man repeated.

Christina stood up straight and puffed out her chest. Redness overcame her olive face as her hands turned to fists. "Not today," she whispered through her clenched jaw. She lunged forward like a charging bull elephant and roared, "this is my house, and you need to get out right now. I'm calling the police!"

The man fell backward as if the sheer force of her words was strong enough to move him. He stopped shouting and looked around. A second later, he dove for a loaf of bread near the toaster and wobbled toward Christina. Christina took two steps back and almost tripped. She caught herself on the counter when the man ran past her out the open door. He missed a step on the stairs and fell onto the driveway near Noah and Maddie, who stood rooted in place as they were told. But at their mother's beckoning wave, both ran past the man and up the stairs to Christina.

The man kneeled and touched the new patch of road rash above his right temple. He leaned on the SUV to regain his footing.

Christina watched him stagger up to the sidewalk and head south. She reached into her purse and retrieved her cell phone. Six minutes later, the police arrived.

The police verified everyone was okay and examined the

scene. Once they completed their investigation, they packed up to leave.

"Do you think you'll catch this guy?" Christina asked.

The officers looked at each other, and the older one spoke. "It's hard to say. Unfortunately, this is more of a problem of homelessness in this area. Even if we catch him, it's not likely he'll be prosecuted."

"He broke into my home. I'm not sure I feel safe living here anymore."

"That's understandable, ma'am. I'm just sharing what we see around here all the time. I can't promise anything, but I don't think that guy will be back. His description fits a man we've crossed a dozen times over the past few years. He's homeless and has a serious substance abuse problem. I'd bet he's on the hunt for another fix, a bite to eat, or a place to crash right now."

Christina pulled her kids close and thanked the officers.

She put a movie in for the kids to help take their minds off the traumatic event they witnessed.

Christina went into her room, closed the door and fell back onto her bed. Her arms stopped trembling and now she was exhausted after all the adrenaline pumped through her body an hour earlier. She wanted to rest, but first Christina wanted to talk to Rey. She texted him and Rey called back twenty minutes later.

"Hey, what's up?" Rey inquired when Christina answered the phone.

All of the emotion bubbled up at once and Christina unloaded the recent event to Rey.

Rey remained silent on his end of the line as he absorbed every detail of Christina's retelling of the events. At the point when the intruder yelled at Christina to leave, Rey spoke.

"What did you do after he yelled at you?"

"I thought about the attack on my mom, and my fear turned to anger, so I yelled back at him. I told him he needed to leave and that I was calling the police. That scared him, and he ran."

The ends of Christina's lips turned upward as she recalled her brave response.

After Christina finished telling Rey her conversation with the police, Rey responded, "I don't like that neighborhood. I wish I would have been there with you. I'm going to see if I can get off early so I can drive down tonight."

"No, don't do that. That's not why I called you at work."

"Why did you call me then?"

"I want you to hurry up and finish the house so we can move back. I hate living in two different houses with two mortgages. I want to move back in soon, but not until all the construction is over. Can you find someone to help you speed it up?"

Rey was silent for a few seconds.

"I'm not going to sleep until I get it done and get you and the kids back up here in Austin with me. Start packing, so you can get back up here as soon as possible."

"Hurry, Rey. We need to be with you."

CHAPTER TWENTY

For the next two weeks, Rey worked on the house before and after work. He had a plan to put the finishing touches on the bathroom and then moving his family into their dream home soon.

At the office, Rey and the Project Second Chance team worked on fine tuning the operating procedures for RIHARP. The team finished the requirements for citizen hosts first but were stuck on how to qualify the inmates. They debated whether they should target inmates without a violent past, were closest to the end of their sentence or the prisoners with the highest likelihood of success as a citizen after they reenter society. After passionate pleas for all options, the project team came to a consensus that RIHARP needed success stories and the likelihood of success as a citizen became the key qualification for inmates. The team outlined the psychological profile, behavior history, and screening questions they envisioned for inmate qualification.

"It's going to take a long time to finalize the entire qualification process by our deadline," Carrie stated after she saw the long list on the white board.

Rey nodded. "I know, but we have to cover all our bases in the qualifying documents or the facilities around Texas won't know how to execute them. It's a lot, but I'm confident we'll get it all done in time."

The following week, the Project Second Chance team prepared to present their rough draft to Deputy Director Scalise. They tested their PowerPoint slides on the screen and rehearsed who would present each slide. When Deputy Director Scalise was over ten minutes late, Rey found his assistant, Annie, pecking at her keyboard outside his office.

"He got called into another meeting with some of the other division directors," the middle-aged woman responded in a pleasant voice.

"Did he say when he may be available? We had a meeting scheduled with him at ten o'clock."

"No, but in the past these emergency director meetings have lasted well into the afternoon so I wouldn't expect to see him today."

"Okay, I'll see if I can get on his calendar tomorrow."

"He did leave a message for you though. He texted me from the meeting."

Rey's eyebrows narrowed.

"Oh, he did?"

"Yes, he said you have one week to finish and present him with the final documents for RIHARP."

"Did you say final documents?"

Annie looked down at her phone. "Yes, he specifically said 'final documents.'"

"That's three weeks earlier than we'd planned. Did he say why?"

"He didn't say, but he asked me put a meeting on your calendar to discuss the presentation in ten days. He said that would give him three days to review it, so he has time to make revisions."

Rey called his own emergency meeting with the Project Second Chance team.

"I have some bad news. We're going to be working late for the next week. The deputy director wants the final report a week from today." The moans from the team was drowned out by Rey's own dread for the earlier deadline. Now he'd have to work late every night and put the remodel of his home on hold. That was an extra week he'd have to wait until he had his family back.

After a week of late nights and Chinese takeout, Rey arrived outside deputy director Scalise's office for his meeting. He motioned to the chair in front of his desk, "Have a seat, Rey."

The deputy director gave his full attention to a handful of papers in front of him. Once he shuffled through them and found the order to his liking, Deputy Director Scalise looked up at Rey. "I've read through all your documentation on how RIHARP will be implemented with the citizen hosts and inmates. It's very thorough and I'm ready to take it to the full committee for approval."

Rey relaxed his shoulders. "Thank you. I appreciate it. It was a real team effort."

"This gives us a great roadmap on how to kick off the beta program with TDCJ staff and employees. During our directors meeting last week, the division directors agreed everyone involved with RIHARP would have to host an inmate so we can all be fully aware of how RIHARP and Sure Cuffs function in a residential environment."

Rey leaned closer to ensure he heard correctly. He turned his right ear to the deputy director. "I'm sorry. Did you say everyone involved with RIHARP will have to host an inmate?"

"Yes, Rey. During the meeting, a recommendation was made that it should be mandatory for everyone involved with this project to host an inmate. All of the directors agreed that if this team is going to promote RIHARP, we need to know firsthand every detail about it."

Rey unfastened another button on his shirt when he felt his body temperature rise and his pulse quicken. He knew this would be a problem for Christina. He didn't think she'd allow a convicted felon to live under the same roof as their two young children. Rey wasn't sure he wanted that either.

"I understand the intent of the directors' decision, but I will have small children living at home again next month. Did any of them discuss the safety impact on families with small children?"

"Yes, we did. It was debated among several directors but then we agreed that ultimately if we are going to recommend this to the citizens of Texas, we all need to have full confidence in everything about this program. That includes families with children. I will be taking an inmate into my home myself."

"But, sir, your children are grown and out of the house, and mine are only six and eight years old. I think the safety threat is a little bit different."

"I understand that this is not the ideal situation. We can't exclude RIHARP from all families with children. It wouldn't be viable if it's just open to single adults and empty nesters. Plus, the directors concluded that participation by TDCJ staff is mandatory. If you want to stay on the Project Second Chance team, you'll have to host an inmate just like the rest of us."

Rey was running out of valid arguments, so he didn't respond.

"Do you no longer believe in RIHARP?" Mr. Scalise asked.

His words hit Rey like a roundhouse punch from a heavyweight boxer. It especially stung because Rey knew he was being hypocritical. At the same time, he could envision the reluctance Christina would have moving back if he suggested they host an inmate. He felt betrayal building inside of him but pushed it back down in front of his supervisor.

"Yes, I still believe in it. It's just going to negatively impact my personal life."

"You can thank your old boss. Lamar said he wanted to be one of the first to volunteer to host an inmate. He also said he thought it would be an excellent idea for everyone on the committee to host an inmate. He said there's no better way to promote a new program to the public then to show that government officials participated in the program first. The directors realized that having TDCJ employees try this first could provide a tremendous opportunity to learn how to improve this program before we release it to the general public."

Rey's stomach turned sour and he stood up. "Thank you, sir. I'll figure out how to make this work."

Rey stumbled out of the office and back to his desk. He loved his job and would do almost anything to keep it. His mind was swimming with questions.

How will Christina react? Am I putting my family in danger? Is Sure Cuffs 100% safe?

Rey had a lot of questions, but he didn't have answers. He rubbed at the back of his neck and then his temples while he stared out over empty cubicles. An hour after the last person on his floor left, Rey packed up his laptop. He was in no hurry to have this conversation with Christina.

Before he arrived at the bank of elevators, Rey passed Lamar's dark office. He stopped and glared at the empty chair.

"Thanks for putting my family in danger."

CHAPTER TWENTY-ONE

Rey decided on the way home to wait until Friday to tell Christina in person. In less than twenty-four hours, he'd be in San Antonio with his family.

After arriving at his old house in the Alamo City, Rey spent time with the kids. He took them to a park two neighborhoods away because it was cleaner. Once they returned from the park, Rey helped Christina with dinner, showered, and read Maddie a bedtime story.

After both kids were asleep, Rey told Christina about the inmate. He was prepared for a fight and defend the necessity of hosting a RIHARP inmate to save his job. However, her reaction surprised him. Christina's lips began to quiver, and she sat down with her face buried in her hands.

Rey moved next to her and put his arm around her. "What's wrong?"

Christina did not answer. Rey asked again and this time she looked up with bloodshot eyes and said, "We can't move back in with you."

Rey stared back at Christina but didn't say anything.

"I'm sorry. I wish I could be more supportive, but you're

inviting danger to live in our home. I don't feel comfortable with that right now."

The grim reality that he was pushing his family away washed over his body like a rogue wave. Hkie kissed Christina on the top of her head and left the room.

Rey fired up his laptop and began to search for a new job. It was his only option. He searched for an hour and found a couple of viable job listings, so he saved them. When Rey arrived back in the bedroom, he saw that Christina was asleep on top of the comforter. She was still dressed with a trail of tears evident on her cheeks like a dry river.

Rey whispered so not to wake her up, "I'm sorry, honey. I'm going to find a new job, so you and the kids can come back home."

For the next week, Rey scoured the internet and applied for every position he thought might grant him an interview. The deadline for him to submit his RIHARP application to host an inmate was two weeks away and he wanted to have a new job in place before he had to make that life-altering decision.

Rey checked his phone throughout the day to see if he received a text or email seeking an interview. He rushed home after work each day to search for additional job opportunities.

One afternoon when Rey was walking back to his office from his lunch break, he heard a ping on his phone. He dug into his pocket and saw it was from one of the companies he'd sent his resume requesting a phone interview. His heart raced with excitement and he quickly responded that he was immediately available for a call.

Two hours later, Rey left his desk and sat in his truck in the TDCJ parking lot to call the person who texted him. It took less than two minutes into the call for Rey to know this position was not going to be the one to save him from RIHARP. It was a road warrior position that required eighty percent travel. Rey knew he didn't want that either. He traveled far less than eighty percent in the Air Force and both Christina and Rey felt that was too much. Rey told the chipper lady on the other end of the line that he couldn't commit to that much travel and thanked her for reaching out to him.

His RIHARP application to host an inmate was due in less than seven days and he didn't have any leads for a new job. His life was coming to a crossroads that he never would have expected when he accepted his manager position two months earlier.

Rey pounded his fist on the steering wheel. "Why does it have to be this way? I can't do this."

The deadline for Rey to submit his RIHARP application passed without his submission. Rey received an invitation from Mr. Scalise's administrative assistant for a meeting later that afternoon. Rey already knew what the meeting was about and was prepared to face the music.

When Rey entered the deputy director's office for the meeting, he slinked across the room to the chair facing his desk. His eyes were fixed on the floor like a mischievous dog waiting for her owner to scold her. The deputy director left his chair and leaned on his desk a few feet in front of Rey.

"What's going on, Rey? You knew the deadline was today and you missed it."

"Yes, sir, I did."

"Do you understand that if you want to be on the Project Second Chance team, that you need to host an inmate within the RIHARP pilot program? I value having you on this team and up until now, I got the impression that you valued being on this team. Is that not true?"

Rey's eyes snapped up from the floor.

"Of course, it's true, I love being part of this team. It's important to me to make a difference for these inmates but the timing is bad for me personally."

"Can I ask why the timing is so bad for you?"

Rey cleared his throat and adjusted his weight in the chair.

"My wife is still living in our old house in San Antonio while I remodeled our current house here. I'm almost done, so they were planning to move back in soon, but now my wife doesn't feel comfortable moving our six and eight-year-old kids back home if an inmate is living there. She's not sure it will be safe."

The deputy director exhaled and crossed his arms.

"I'm sorry to hear that and I understand the concern, but we can't make an exception for one person. All of us have our concerns about taking an inmate into our home but we believe in what we're doing, and all need to make sacrifices for the greater good."

The deputy director moved back behind his desk and sat down. He leaned forward in his chair. "I'll give you a couple more days to think about it but if you don't have your application for a RIHARP inmate in by noon on Thursday you'll leave me with no choice. I'll have to process you back into your previous position, compensation, and supervisor."

Rey's eyes widened.

"I'll have to report to Lamar Taylor again?"

"Yes, and you're lucky to even have that option because they never filled your old position. HR put a hold on it after we added your current position of special projects manager. The other option is complete separation from TDCJ. I really hope you'll reconsider your decision over the weekend and submit your application so you can remain a member of this team. The ball is in your court and those are the two remaining options if your application is not submitted on time."

Rey's face blanched as he sunk into the chair. The mere thought of reporting to Lamar again was enough to make the hair stand up on the back of his neck. After a few seconds of uncomfortable silence, the deputy director spoke.

"Give it some thought, Rey. I believe you're not giving yourself and your family enough credit. You're a former corrections officer and can handle any inmate that's outfitted with Sure Cuffs. Give your options some serious consideration. Just remember that if your application is not submitted by noon on Thursday that you'll no longer be on the Project Second Chance team or reporting to me. You'll be back in your former position or terminated from TDCJ if you choose not to accept your old position by the end of the day. I think that would be a shame, because your vision is really needed."

Rey left the office early and called Christina on the way home.

"Can you take the kids over to your parent's house and come up here tonight? We need to talk."

Christina arrived three hours later. Rey had takeout ready on plates in the kitchen, so they ate first. After Christina took the disposable plates to the trash, she moved to the couch and Rey followed.

"So, what's on your mind?"

"I've been given an ultimatum at work and I want discuss it with you."

Her eyes narrowed and Rey began. He shared the entire conversation with the deputy director.

"So my options are to host an inmate, get fired, or to report to Lamar again. That's like asking if I want to cut off my left arm, my right arm, or both. I don't like any of those options."

Christina stood up and stared at Rey with hands on her hips. He guessed she was going through the same shock he did a few hours earlier when these options were presented to him.

"Honestly, I'd rather be unemployed then report to Lamar again, but I know we don't have anything left in our savings and can barely pay for both houses and medical bills today."

Rey took a step closer to Christina and lowered his voice. "Would you at least consider moving back here if I requested a minimum-security inmate, so the physical threat of harm isn't so great to our family?"

Christina paced in the family room. She started to speak and then would stop and start pacing again. Suddenly she stopped in front of Rey and pulled him down to sit on the couch next to her. She looked Rey deep in his eyes.

"I don't want you to be unemployed and I don't want you to

have to report to Lamar again. Both of those are terrible options for you and our family. I'll agree to host an inmate as long as you request a minimum-security prisoner."

Christina got up and left the room. Rey watched her leave and then fell back into the cushions. Maybe he could make this work. He'd submit the application for a RIHARP inmate on time and hope they give him a minimum-security prisoner. Rey closed his eyes and prayed.

This was Rey's first glimmer of hope since hearing that he'd have to host an inmate.

CHAPTER TWENTY-TWO

Thursday morning, Rey submitted his application to host a RIHARP inmate twenty minutes before the deadline. For the next two weeks Rey and the rest of the members of the Project Second Chance team awaited their assignments. To avoid potential bias, a committee based in the Huntsville facility outside of Houston was created to assign the RIHARP inmates. That way nobody from Austin could be influenced to assign an inmate based on the person or position held by another TDCJ employee in their office. Rey was glad Lamar wasn't going to be involved in the inmate assignments.

Two weeks from the day Rey submitted his RIHARP application, Deputy Director Scalise called a meeting to distribute the assignment letters and review them as a team. Once everyone was seated in the conference room, he handed out each envelope to every member of the Project Second Chance team. He gave a quick preamble to what they should expect but Rey wasn't listening.

Was it someone with multiple drug possession charges? Or would he get somebody in for grand theft larceny? He wanted to tear the envelope open as soon as it landed on the large boardroom table in front of him, but he waited for the deputy director to give the word.

"Okay, go ahead and open your envelope."

All the team members tore open their envelopes and yanked out the letter. The hum of the fluorescent lights was the only sound as everyone read the bio of the inmates they were assigned. After a minute, some of them put down their letters and looked around the room with a smile at the other team members. Rey did neither. He re-read the letter in disbelief.

He was assigned a maximum-security prisoner from Huntsville who was convicted of murder. After Rey read it the second time, he put the letter down and excused himself. He went into the bathroom stall, closed the door and dry heaved. The absolute worst assignment that Rey could think of was given to him.

Fifteen minutes later, Rey left the stall, washed his face and went back to his desk. He grabbed his backpack and told the admin assistant he wasn't feeling well and left for home.

Ray felt lightheaded during the longest twenty-minute commute home since he moved to Austin. *How did this happen?*

He went into his bedroom and collapsed on his bed. Solutions to his latest setback evaded his consciousness as he stared at the ceiling.

Ping.

Rey turned to his phone lying next to Christina's pillow. It was a text from Christina.

Did you find out who the inmate is yet?

He didn't have the energy to discuss his incredible bad fortune with the inmate he was assigned. Plus, Rey knew he needed to have this conversation in person, so he ignored the text.

"I'll text her later," Rey said aloud as he pulled the pillow over his face.

Thirty minutes later Rey rose from bed and looked at his watch, calculating that it was after ten now in Guam. Rey found his brother's phone number in his contacts and hit send.

"Hey, Rey, what's happening?" Carlos bellowed from seven thousand miles away like he was in the next room.

"Oh, a lot's happening. What's up with you? Are you and Alani spending all your free time on the beach?"

The brothers caught up on work and families for the next five minutes.

"I do have a specific question for you. I need some advice."

"Ok, shoot," Carlos replied.

Rey explained his new position, RIHARP and the situation with Christina and the kids living in their old house until their new one was ready.

"I don't know what to do. I feel like I'm in a lose - lose situation."

The line was silent for a few seconds until Carlos replied. "I know how important your family is, but I also know that you've wanted to make big changes with inmates since you and Papa came back from Norway. I can only think of one way out of this. Make Christina feel safe with the inmate living there."

"Sounds great. Would you care to share how I could do that with a guy convicted of murder bunking down the hall from Noah and Maddie?"

Carlos laughed. "I didn't say it would be easy, but I'd start with trying to make Christina part of the process. I don't know what this guy is like, but maybe he's reformed. Maybe he's no longer the monster you think he could be. See if Christina and the kids can meet him and maybe he won't be as intimidating as you think it may be for her."

"Hmm." Rey tapped his index finger on his lips. "That's not such a dumb idea, Carlos. I'll see if Christina can meet him when he arrives and possibly even bring the kids."

"I appreciate the compliment, little bro. You can thank me later."

"If it works, I'll definitely owe you a big thank you. When are you coming back to the states?"

"I'm not sure yet. Alani is planning a trip to Honolulu for her parents' fortieth wedding anniversary so that may be our big trip this year. If something comes up that brings me stateside, I'll let you know."

Rey found a new bounce in his step after the call with Carlos. Would Christina be okay with this inmate if she met him?

It was Rey's only chance to keep his job and get his family back. He texted Christina and told her he was going to come down on Saturday. Rey needed an extra day to work on this pitch. This would be his biggest selling job ever to Christina.

CHAPTER TWENTY-THREE

When Rey arrived in San Antonio, the house was empty. Christina was picking up the kids from a neighbor's birthday party. He sat down at the table and put his headphones on. The Three Tenors belted out notes that took Rey five thousand miles across the Atlantic to the Berlin Opera House where he heard his first opera. He didn't understand the words, but he could feel their emotion. It penetrated deep inside his bones and made him feel light enough to fly away like a bird. He was hooked and opera music has been a source of inspiration ever since that night in Berlin. Rey needed every ounce of inspiration he could muster for his next conversation with Christina.

His family arrived, chattering happily together. Christina gave Rey a hug and kiss after both kids exchanged hugs with their father. Noah and Maddie ran into the family room to play and Christina put her purse on the counter.

"You sounded like you had something urgent to tell me on the phone. What is it?"

"You should probably start a movie for the kids," Rey suggested.

Christina stared at Ray for a few seconds before she gathered the kids in front of the TV and started their favorite movie, *The*

Lion King, for the billionth time. Ray knew that would buy them over an hour before the kids came looking for them.

Rey motioned for Christina to follow him into the kitchen. He sat at the kitchen table behind a manila file folder. Christina inched down into her chair when she noticed the file.

"Is that the inmate?"

"Yes, and it's not what I was expecting."

Christina kept her eyes locked on Rey as he pushed the file folder across the table. She opened the folder and looked down at the cover of an inmate profile. Rey saw Christina wince at the sight of the inmate's picture. As she read the letter, he watched her carefully, sensing where her eyes were on the page based on her expressions. When she narrowed her eyebrows and deep wrinkles formed above her glasses, Christina closed the file.

"This isn't what I agreed to. A murderer from a maximum-security prison? Plus, he has a charge of assaulting a minor. This is not the type of person I feel comfortable living alongside under our roof with our children."

Rey could only stare back in silence. He had no words of justification. He was in far too deep to turn back now.

"We have to give this a shot, Christina. My job depends on it."

"Have you told them you'll have small children living in the house? Tell them you can't take this inmate."

Ray looked down at the table and didn't respond. Christina stood up and moved to the counter. She leaned against it and raked her fingers through her hair.

Rey's neck and cheeks flushed red. The conversation was not going as planned.

"What if you meet the inmate when he arrives, and he's reformed or at least makes you feel comfortable living in our Austin house? Would you at least consider that?"

Christina let out a long sigh, "He's a convicted murderer. Nothing makes me comfortable about that. I can't think about anything else right now."

Rey dropped his head. He had no rebuttal to the fact that his assigned inmate had committed serious crimes in the past.

Christina stormed out of the kitchen. He heard the bedroom door shut. Rey sat at the kitchen table in silence until *The Lion King* was over.

The next morning Rey woke up early. Light from the approaching sun was barely evident in the eastern sky. He decided to go for a quick climb at his favorite spot a half hour northeast of San Antonio. He returned after eight o'clock and Christina was sitting up in bed.

"Couldn't sleep?" Rey whispered.

"No, I've got too much on my mind."

"Me, too. I went climbing this morning to clear my head. Part of me wishes I would have just tried harder to make an impact as a CO down here. This new position has not turned out like I thought it would. I wouldn't have taken it if I knew I was forcing my family to live ninety miles from me for over a year."

Christina looked up, "Don't blame yourself for this. I also wanted you to get a new job and move to Austin. We both wanted all the possibilities your new position could bring us."

Rey nodded as he grabbed a towel for the shower. When he got out, Christina was waiting for him.

"I've decided I'll be there when the inmate arrives, but not the kids. I'll have my parents watch them so I can stay a couple of nights. Let's see how we all feel after we actually meet."

Rey couldn't believe his ears. This was the best response he could've hoped for.

"Thank you."

Rey returned to Austin and he moved his stuff out of the guest room. It was the first bedroom in the hallway and right across from a full bathroom. The kids would have to pass the room every time they went to or from their bedrooms when they come back home, but it kept the inmate away from their rooms at the end of the hallway at night. This was one of the requirements from

Christina. The inmate would not be allowed to go past his bathroom. Ever. He would be restricted to his end of the hallway.

Rey tested the TV remote, checked the clothes in the dresser and straightened the comforter. He stood in the center of the room and did a complete turn. Was a convicted murderer really going to be living in here next week?

Rey dropped back onto the bed and sat with his feet on the floor. He stared at the wooden planks he exposed months ago. On his way out, Rey turned to scan the room one last time before he flipped off the light switch.

"Ready or not, an inmate will be living in here soon."

CHAPTER TWENTY-FOUR

After his one o'clock meeting on Wednesday ended, Rey left work. It would be his last day in the office until his inmate was acclimated to life as a house guest. The RIHARP team established a rule that TDCJ hosts would work from home to ensure a smooth transition from life behind bars to one of relative freedom for the inmates.

Rey felt the tension as soon as he entered the house. Neither he nor Christina said much until three thirty. At that time, they both went out on the front porch to wait for their new guest.

Rey peered down the street without blinking, his chest growing tighter every minute. Christina paced on the grey wood planks. They both froze when two black GMC Yukon SUVs pulled in front of their house and parked.

Three TDCJ corrections officers and a man in a suit emerged. Sure Cuffs creator and CEO of Sectronix, John Nickerson, was the man in the suit. He greeted Rey and Christina at the end of the sidewalk while two officers stood by the rear passenger door. John extended his hand to Christina.

"Hello Mrs. Mendoza, I'm John Nickerson with Sectronix and I work with your husband. I'll be guiding you through the exchange process today." He turned to the SUVs and then back to

Rey and Christina. "Are you ready to meet your RIHARP inmate?"

Christina did not respond at first, her eyes were fixed on the passenger door of the GMC Yukon. Eventually, she turned and said, "Let's do this."

John nodded to the officer near the passenger door and he opened it.

Rey first noticed the thinning blond buzz-cut hair. Then he noticed the tattoos jutting from beneath his orange prison jumpsuit on his hands and neck. Rey guessed the inmate was three or four inches shorter than him and appeared to be well-built. It was clear he spent some time hitting the weights in the yard.

John returned from the vehicle with the inmate. Christina took a step back and moved halfway behind Rey.

"Mr. and Mrs. Mendoza, this is David Kimbell."

David looked Rey in the eyes for a brief second, glanced at Christina, then looked down. "Hello, sir. Hello, ma'am." He spoke with a raspy voice that signaled decades of smoking.

"Hello."

Meeting a new house guest is awkward, Rey mused. It was like a blind date, but instead of getting set up with the perfect match you've dreamt about, you get a man tried and convicted of killing other human beings.

After a few seconds of silence, John suggested that they go inside.

David met with the other officers in the kitchen to begin his transition process. Christina and Rey led John to the small dining room and sat first. John squeezed on the opposite side of the table. John had a binder with colorful flyers and pamphlets. He removed a small stack of papers from his binder and began, "Mr. and Mrs. Mendoza, I'm here today to give you all the details on hosting an inmate through the RIHARP program."

John outlined the required living arrangements, reporting parameters, and legal liabilities.

Christina nodded, murmuring how thorough the explanations

were, and Rey couldn't help smiling. His team had worked hard to cover all the bases.

"Rey, I realize you have a good understanding of Sure Cuffs, but it's important for both of you to understand everything about this technology."

John stood up to demonstrate.

"It works by inserting ten rice-sized transmitter chips under the skin of each RIHARP inmate. They're located on each side in their inner knee, thigh, upper hip area, elbow and in the palm of their hand near their thumbs."

John extended one arm and pointed to the base of his thumb in the palm of his hand.

"It's placed right about here."

"This placement is important because these ten chips, when activated, secure the inmate's knees together while bringing their arms and hands in tight next to their body. Kind of like a virtual straitjacket so they are completely immobilized. The inmates will remain in this position until Sure Cuffs are deactivated on your smartphone app or by a TDCJ officer. The app notifies a dispatcher at Sectronix when Sure Cuffs are activated and we'll notify local authorities if necessary."

John pointed to the brochure he'd given them.

Christina slid the glossy booklet in front of her and skimmed through a few pages.

"In order to activate Sure Cuffs, you need to use the smartphone app."

After Christina closed the booklet, John rose from his chair and said, "Okay, let's get started."

He pushed a large binder labeled *RIHARP Inmate Profile: David Kimbell* toward Christina.

"This binder contains all the information on Mr. Kimbell. It contains his personal history and his psychological profile. I recommend reading this information as soon as possible so you are aware of his background, habits, and everything else that can help make hosting this inmate a smooth transition."

"I'll let the two of you look this over for a bit while I check on the inmate transition team."

Neither one opened the binder.

"What's wrong?" Rey asked.

"This just got real."

"What do you mean?"

"This is no longer just a discussion about a potential inmate living here. A convicted murderer and child abuser is in our kitchen right now getting the ground rules for living here. It's creepy."

"You said you would give this a try."

"I am, but I'm not sure how comfortable I'll be with this man and our kids living under the same roof," Christina shot back.

Rey stared at Christina for several seconds before turning to the binder. He flipped past several pages of counselor's reports, prison photos and police reports from David's youth.

John returned to the dining room.

"They just wrapped up with Mr. Kimbell. Do either of you have any questions for me before we finish here?"

Christina shook her head and looked down at the table.

"We're good for now, but I'll contact you if we have any questions," Rey replied.

John followed the officers out of the house. He gave the house one final look before he disappeared back into one of the black GMC SUVs.

After John and the rest of the TDCJ team left, Christina went into their bedroom and closed the door.

Rey was alone with his new house guest.

He motioned for David to follow him down the hallway, then led the way into the guest room. "This will be your room. Your bathroom is just across the hall. You have your own TV and we set you up with Internet access on that laptop on the dresser. It's monitored by the TDCJ so don't try to do anything you wouldn't do in Huntsville."

"You used to be a prison guard?"

Rey paused the walking tour of his home. "Yes, I was. Why?"

"It's not gonna be like that around here is it?"

Rey tilted his head and took a step closer to David. "If you're asking if there's going to be rules, then yes, it will be like that."

"I understand rules. I'm just wondering if you're going to treat me like a prisoner or a guest in your home?"

Rey stared at the fidgety man in his guestroom for several seconds before responding.

"If we come to think of you as a guest, we'd be happy."

"Unwelcome guest?"

Rey took a step closer to David and locked eyes with him.

"That depends on you."

The tour continued throughout the cozy one-story home. He showed David the family room, a small dining room, and the kitchen. It ended back in the guest bedroom.

"You have free rein everywhere inside the house except our bedroom and the kid's rooms. Never go past your bathroom down this hallway."

David stood with a blank look on his face.

"Do you understand? Never go past your bathroom."

"I get it."

Rey crossed the room and opened the door to the tiny closet. "TDCJ provided some civilian clothes in the dresser and a pair of shoes next to the bed. We picked up some additional clothes for you that are in this closet. They should be your size."

Rey turned on the TV and tossed the remote control in the middle of the queen-size bed. He strolled over to the door and leaned up against the threshold. "Do you have any questions?"

David moved a few shirts in the closet from the left side to the right and turned to the TV. "How many channels do I have?"

"I don't know exactly. It's cable so you have all the same channels we do. I'd guess about seventy-five."

"When can I go outside?"

"I'm glad you asked. You said you understood the rules so remember this is like house arrest. You can't go outside unless my wife or I give you permission. If we give you permission, we need to always be outside with you. If you try to sneak out, you'll get caught and shipped back to Huntsville to serve out your remaining sentence and then some for trying to escape. You've got a unique opportunity with RIHARP, don't ruin it."

"Yes, sir. I understand," David replied.

Rey nodded. He'd met hundreds, if not thousands of inmates before so he felt he was a good judge of character. David's politeness was genuine, not sneering or manipulative. He seemed a little sad and quiet, but overall, David made a positive first impression on Rey.

He could only hope Christina would warm to David.

CHAPTER TWENTY-FIVE

The next morning, Christina trudged to the kitchen for her first cup of coffee. She leapt up and took several steps back when she noticed David sitting at the kitchen table. He was drinking a cup of coffee with no shirt on. After a second look, she realized he was wearing only his boxer shorts.

Christina bolted from the kitchen. "Rey, get up!"

Rey shot up. He grabbed onto the dresser to balance himself. "What is it?"

"It's David. He's in the kitchen."

Rey wrinkled his nose and rubbed his eyes. "It's okay for him to have free access anywhere in this house except for our end of the hallway. That's what we agreed to."

"I know. He's in the kitchen and he's in just his boxer shorts. Nothing else. He's got tattoos all over his body. I don't want him walking around the house like that."

Rey put one hand up in surrender. "Okay, okay. I'll go talk to him. "

Rey threw on a shirt and jeans. He found David still sitting at the kitchen table.

"I'm sorry I scared your wife," he said. "I don't think she was expecting to see me sitting here so early in the morning. I guess I'm just used to getting up early. "

"Like we talked about last night, you can come and go in here as you please. The problem is that you barely have any clothes on. We want you to be comfortable, but don't you think that's maybe a little too comfortable?"

David looked down at his mostly naked body as if he needed to confirm the accusation himself. He chuckled. "I guess you may be right. I'll go throw some clothes on."

"I'd appreciate that."

When Rey returned to the bedroom, Christina was standing next to the bed with a look of concern.

"He's going to put some clothes on now and will have something on at all times in the future outside of his room."

"I hope so. I can't imagine if Maddie or Noah would have saw him like that. They'd be freaked out by all those tattoos."

Rey dropped to the bed next to Christina.

"When do you think it'd be okay to introduce the kids to David?"

Christina sighed and shook her head. "It was pretty alarming to see him. I don't want to introduce the kids right now."

Rey scooted closer to Christina. "How about next Tuesday? You can bring the kids right after they get out of school. That will give me almost a week to better understand David and help him assimilate into life outside of prison."

"Next Tuesday doesn't work for me."

"Why not?" Rey asked.

Christina sat next to Rey on the bed. "Because I have an interview at North East School District. I planned to tell you when I got here. A second-grade teacher at Castle Hills elementary is expected to go on maternity leave in the fall and her current sub is relocating to Seattle. It's a temporary full-time position in a great school district."

Rey lowered his head, "That means it will be even longer

before you move back. I was hoping you'd wait until I figured all this out."

"I'd like to move back up here with the kids if everything can be ironed out, but we also need to be realistic about our expenses. We are paying for two houses, so we need two incomes. Even when we move back, I'm going to need to work."

"That's fair, but let's at least introduce the kids to David first before we make any long-term decisions."

"I'll bring them up next Thursday. They have early release so I can get here by three o'clock."

Rey walked Christina to her SUV and watched her drive away. He jogged back to the house as soon as she turned the corner. He had eight days to develop a relationship with David so his family would feel comfortable moving back in.

This was his only shot to get his family back before summer.

Rey worked from home while he got to know David and his habits. He found out that David loved his morning coffee and sitting outside after his third cup. In the afternoon, David watched Judge Judy for hours. David was constantly hungry and wanted to snack all day rather than eat a meal, a habit he told Rey he developed years ago when he chose to quit smoking in prison. Any money he accumulated, he spent in the prison commissary on canned meat and blocks of cheese to keep him full between meals.

Rey found one of David's less endearing habits was his nagging persistence. He was worse than Rey's six and eight-year-old kids begging for sweets. David would linger and ask repeatedly until Rey was forced to scold him. His most frequent request was to go outside and sit on the porch. Rey assumed it was due to David's extended stay in his tight quarters at Huntsville. Although it required Rey to stop what he was doing to escort David to the front porch, he was typically accommodating of his request to go outside. It was something Rey figured he'd want to do too if he had been behind bars like David.

Rey felt more comfortable with David every day. He prayed David would be on his best behavior when Christina showed up with the kids later that afternoon.

David was in his room when the kids arrived. In typical fashion, they raced through the door and found their father. Hugs and kisses where exchanged and then they ran off to their rooms in the *new house* that they've barely lived in. Neither one noticed the guest bedroom door was shut.

When Christina arrived in the house, she was all business. She wanted to introduce the kids as soon as possible.

First, Christina gathered both kids with Rey in their bedroom. "We have a new friend who's going to be living here for a while."

"Who is he?" Maddie asked.

"He's a friend of Dad. His name is David and he's going to be living in the guestroom."

"How long is he going to be here?"

Christina turned to Rey. He wished he had a good answer to that question. They were told that they needed to keep David long enough to verify that the RIHARP program works, so no firm timeframe was provided.

Rey shrugged. "I don't know. He's probably going to be living here a little bit."

Christina instructed her children to follow her and she led them down the hall toward David's door. Rey stayed back at the end of the hall.

Christina gently knocked with both of her children standing in front of her. A few seconds later the door opened abruptly. Both children darted behind their mother at the sight of the stranger.

David chuckled and looked down at the two children clinging tight to their mother's shirt. "Hello, there."

His raspy voice didn't help reduce the fear in Noah and Maddie.

Christina pushed them to her side. "This is David. He's the guest that we talked about a few minutes ago who's going to be living with us."

Noah looked up at Christina. "He's dad's friend?"

Christina looked at David and then back down at her son. "They met through work."

Christina turned back to David. "This is my daughter Maddie and my son Noah. Say hello to Mr. David."

Both kids said "Hello, Mr. David" in unison.

"Can we go now?" Maddie asked.

At their mother's nod, both kids ran off past Rey into the family room, leaving Christina alone with David. Rey mirrored Christina's crossed arms and they shared forced smiles.

Christina started to turn away but stopped herself. "Rey told you about the rule not to go down near any of the bedrooms, right?"

David nodded.

"Okay, that's very important that you don't go down the hallway past your own room. That's the one rule that's important to me."

"Yes, ma'am. I won't, "

"Thank you. I appreciate it."

Christina headed to the kitchen and Rey followed

"That wasn't so bad was it?" he asked.

"Not horrible, but the kids seemed apprehensive of him."

"Do you feel comfortable enough to move the kids back up here after school is out?"

"Are you completely done with the remodel?"

Rey inhaled deeply and let it out, "Not yet. I've had so much else to do, but I'll hit it hard now since I'm going to be working from home for a while."

"Why don't you have David help you?"

"I don't think he knows anything about construction. It would just slow me down if I had to show him how to do everything," Rey protested.

"Or it could help speed things up. Get him involved, Rey. It can't hurt."

Christina reached for her purse, slung it over her shoulder and yelled for the kids in one fluid motion. "Noah and Maddie, time to leave."

"Wait," Rey said. "How did the interview go?"

Christina put her purse back down and smiled. "I think it went well. They have several candidates to interview so they said they'd make a decision before the end of the school year. I should hear back in a few weeks."

"I hate to say it, but I hope you don't get it."

Christina shook her head and shouldered her purse again. "Thanks for all the confidence and support."

Christina yelled again for the kids, this time in a tone they understood contained a high degree of risk if they didn't comply.

Rey moved in front of Christina and put his hands on her waist. "I'm sorry, I didn't mean it that way. I just hope you can move back up here soon so you don't have to get a job in San Antonio. I miss you, Maddie and Noah. I want you back here as soon as possible."

"Finish the remodel and we can talk about it."

The kids came for their good-bye hugs and kisses, then they left with Christina for San Antonio.

The moment they pulled out of the driveway, Rey grabbed his tool belt and went back to the hallway bathroom. He chipped away at the old mosaic tiles on the floor.

Rey worked alone for hours. It was something he'd get used to.

CHAPTER TWENTY-SIX

For the next two weeks, Rey was confined to his house. He didn't have anyone else to watch his inmate if he left and Rey grew more impatient with the same daily routine. During his scheduled FaceTime call with Christina and the kids, he tried to be upbeat about it all. Christina continued to be cagey about the full-time teaching job she'd applied for, saying next to nothing about her interview. Rey suspected there was more going on than she was sharing with him.

Rey's father called regularly to report his progress with the new diet and exercise regime the doctor ordered, but Rey knew it was mostly a cover to check up on how living with an inmate was working out. Rey talked about David's eating habits more than anything else. To tell Rodolfo how trapped he felt would mean revealing Christina wasn't here as back-up, and he didn't want to tax Papa's weak heart.

After sitting on the porch with David one morning, Rey stayed outside after David went back inside. He thought about his current situation.

It's like David and I switched places. He has this newly acquired freedom he's learning to enjoy and I'm more restricted and isolated than I've ever been. I didn't see this coming with a RIHARP inmate.

Minutes later, Rey went into the bathroom to make progress on the remodel. He thought more about potential solutions as he peeled off small strips of wallpaper from the bathroom wall. After removing one long, productive strip behind the sink, he jumped up.

"I've got it."

Rey fired up his laptop and composed an email to Deputy Director Scalise and all other RIHARP hosts. He suggested that they all bring their inmates into the TDCJ office during their first monthly review meeting in early June for a group session with counselors. All the counselors have the Sure Cuffs app on their phones so they could watch the inmates without the hosts. Rey hit send and waited for the responses.

The next morning, Rey opened his email and pumped his fist. Everyone liked his idea and Deputy Director Scalise even said he'd coordinate the room and counselors with the appropriate directors.

Freedom was in sight again for Rey.

He dedicated several hours a day to working remotely with the Project Second Chance team and less on the home remodel. Rey also spent a lot of time responding to David's requests for food or outdoor entertainment. If felt like David was standing in front of him with a request for something every half hour. Rey knew he had to try something new to keep David occupied or he'd never get anything done.

Rey sat and watched David devour his second sandwich before three o'clock in the afternoon. An idea hit, so Rey stood up and snapped his fingers. "Netflix!"

David stopped chewing and with a mouth full of peanut butter and jelly, asked, "What did you say?"

"Have you ever watched a movie on Netflix?"

David shook his head and resumed chewing.

"Follow me."

Rey led David into the guest room. He used the remote control to type into the search bar and a list of action movies appeared on the TV screen. "You can search for a movie or entire season of TV shows. It's all covered with my monthly subscription."

A wide smile appeared on David's unshaven face. "I've heard of Netflix but have never seen it. I still can't believe you don't have to use a VHS tape or DVD or anything."

"Watch as much as you like. Binge watch something with several seasons."

David did not respond. He was already scrolling through all the new releases.

For the rest of the week, David only asked to go outside after his morning coffee and after dinner. Rey got more done that week than the previous three combined.

The day of the first monthly review meeting arrived, when the Project Second Chance team would gather all TDCJ employees hosting a RIHARP inmate to discuss how the program was working. Rey secured David in the back seat of his truck. The sight of Noah's booster seat sent a momentary burst of sadness over Rey, but the sense of freedom to leave his house won over his emotions.

Rey maintained his smile all the way to the TDCJ office. He also kept the Sure Cuffs app open on his phone in the seat next to him the entire trip just in case David tried to make a daring escape at a stop light.

Rey escorted David to the conference room with all the counselors. He was one of the first to arrive, but soon a dozen inmates would fill the room in the next half hour.

Once Rey reached his desk, he sat in his chair and stared at the screen. It had never felt so good to be at work. He opened his file of discussion questions for the meeting and proofread it for the fifth time. He wanted this first meeting—focused on gathering feedback from all the hosts and tracking the pilot program's progress—to go as smoothly as possible.

Rey arrived early to the meeting and watched eleven other

TDCJ employees enter the room and take their seats. Lamar Taylor, Rey's former boss, was the last to sit down.

Rey opened the meeting by reading the RIHARP incident reports he and Deputy Director Scalise received over the past thirty days. Other than a heated argument or a fist through a wall, RIHARP was off to a promising start the first month.

After he read the reports, Rey asked every host to share what was working well, what was broken and overall suggestions for improvement. The Project Second Chance team took copious notes of the suggestions.

Near the end of the hour, Rey turned to the deputy director. "I don't have any further questions, do you?"

"No, this has been helpful feedback. I thank you again for your participation in the RIHARP test and your commitment to finding new ways to improve our corrections system."

Everyone got up and left, but Lamar leaned back in his chair. Rey finished jotting down the last of his notes when he saw Lamar staring at him with a grin.

"How's your inmate working out, Rey?"

"Fine. How about your inmate?"

"He's a dream." Lamar said in his slow, Oklahoma drawl. "He was doing time in a minimum-security facility for multiple counts of check fraud. A real threat to society. I think he's more afraid of me than I am of him."

"Wow, that does sound like a dream," Rey said as he stood up and moved toward the exit.

Lamar leaned forward over the table. "How do you like having a convicted murderer living with you?"

Rey stopped and turned around.

I didn't tell anyone Lamar knows about David's conviction. How could he know that?

Lamar flashed a sadistic smirk.

Rey took several steps toward Lamar. "What do you know about my inmate?"

Lamar stood up and began to walk away.

"What do you know?" Rey demanded.

Lamar turned and approached Rey. "I have a lot of friends all over the criminal justice system. It's best not to get on my bad side. Know what I mean?" Lamar bumped into Rey, knocking him back a couple of steps as he walked by.

Rey watched him leave and was too stunned to say anything. If Lamar had tampered with the process, that was a pretty egregious ethics violation. Rey wondered if he ought to report it to the deputy director. How could he prove it, though? Still, he couldn't get Lamar's words out of his head. What did Lamar know that Rey didn't about David?

The questions swirling in Rey's mind was interrupted when someone stopped by to ask if he wanted to join them for lunch.

He shook his head. "No. Maybe next time."

Rey looked at his watch and realized that he had limited time with a chaperone for David. He grabbed his keys and ran errands for two hours. When Rey returned to the TDCJ office with a truck full of groceries, the counselors were waiting impatiently for him to take David. He was the last one in the conference room. Rey felt a hint of guilt for making them babysit his inmate while he got groceries, but the thought of eating something different quickly quelled any guilt.

Lamar's comments resurfaced in Rey's mind. He'd studied David's inmate history and knew of his convictions but didn't know the whole story behind the murder charge. His curiosity grew like storm clouds on a July afternoon in Austin.

He considered asking David, but never summoned the courage. Plus, his mind was on getting the house ready for Christina and the kids. School was out and Christina was bringing them up for a week to stay together in Austin. He expected her to have some news by now about the full-time teaching job she'd been offered.

Rey cleaned up all the construction mess to ensure dust would not be a problem for Noah. He waited for them to pull up in the driveway and opened the door so they could rush out of the SUV like an avalanche of excitement.

The re-introduction of David to Christina and the kids in the kitchen contained several long pauses of silence.

Rey broke the awkward moment. "Maddie, Noah go check out your rooms. They're totally different from the last time you were here."

They ran out of the room and David took it as his cue to depart the kitchen.

Rey held Christina tight for over a minute. He pulled away and asked, "When do you have to give them an answer if you'll accept the offer?"

Christina raised on her tiptoes and gave Rey a quick peck on the lips.

"Not now. Let's just enjoy our time together for the next week and then we can discuss work."

Rey smiled. "Okay. Enjoy we will."

He bent over and cradled Christina's legs with one arm while he leaned her back into his other arm. He carried her like a firefighter out of the kitchen and into the family room.

"Welcome home, Mrs. Mendoza." He set her down gently on the couch.

The sound of her giggles tickled his ears. It was the most beautiful sound he'd heard in years.

CHAPTER TWENTY-SEVEN

Rey, Christina, and the kids enjoyed themselves for the next two days. David wasn't involved much. He started to binge watch a new series on Netflix and was mostly nestled on his bed with his eyes glued to the TV screen.

Rey sensed that Christina and the kids were getting used to David's presence. That would be a big step in convincing Christina to decline the job offer and move back up with the kids.

On the third night, Rey read both kids a bedtime story. Once they fell asleep, he invited Christina to join him on the patio to enjoy the cool night breeze after a warm June day. She agreed and closed her book.

Rey told Christina about Lamar's comments in the conference room. "It's been eating at me ever since. Not just that Lamar somehow tampered with what was supposed to be an impartial process. I still don't know the story of how David ended up in prison and that's bothering me."

Christina nodded.

"I want to invite David to join us out here tonight."

"The three of us?" she asked.

"Yes. I have some things I want to ask him, and I'd like for you to be there with me when I do."

"What are you going to ask him?"

"I want to know what he did to end up in Huntsville. I know he's in for three counts of murder, but I want to know details and I'd like to hear it from him."

"Okay, but can I ask him?"

Rey cocked his head. "I wasn't sure you'd want to know more about what he did."

"I've been dying to find out more since I read his profile."

Rey nodded and then left the front porch.

Tap. Tap. Tap.

Rey knocked on David's door and extended the invitation to join Christina and him on the front porch. David accepted Rey's invitation without hesitation. A minute later, each selected a chair on the patio. They all sat quietly as neighbors walked their dogs and cars whirred past.

Christina and Rey exchanged a couple of quick glances.

Christina nodded and spoke first. "David, what did you do to get sentenced to prison for thirty years?"

Rey squirmed at the abrupt and direct question. He looked over at David, whose mouth was open in shock.

Rey moved to the edge of his seat and leaned forward. He could be on David in less than a second if needed.

David's open mouth turned to a smile and then a deep laugh. "I was wondering when someone was going to ask me why I was locked up."

Christina returned a faint smile. "I didn't want to be rude, but now that you've been here over a month, I thought it was a good time to ask."

David leaned forward and looked over both shoulders as if verifying nobody else was on the porch. "Well, I didn't have the easiest life growing up. My dad was a junkie and he beat me and my brothers when he wasn't passed out as far back as I could remember. I moved out as soon as I graduated from high school and bounced around a bunch of jobs. I caught a break with a construction company after I turned twenty-two, so I bought a bike. It was an old hog, but it ran well."

Christina furrowed her brow. "A hog?"

"Yeah, you know, a Harley. I spent every penny I had to buy it. I went out for a drink by myself one night after work at a biker bar near my apartment and met some other guys. They all rode too, so I hooked up with their club. A few weeks later, I found out they were all involved with meth. They were dealing all around Houston. I tried it one night and I was hooked. I was dealing with them a few weeks later."

David took a long drink of lemonade.

"A year or so later, one of our guys got jumped during a bad deal. They left him for dead. He was in a coma when we got to the hospital to see him. The guys got all fired up about making someone pay, so I drove down to the same neighborhood with two of my boys. I was driving our friends' Chrysler New Yorker. It was at least ten years old and as big as a boat. I pulled up in this tank on the same corner where my friend got jumped. A group of guys approached our car and out of nowhere someone in the back seat opened fire with an AK-47. I didn't even turn around. I heard the guys outside returning fire so I floored it and got out of there as fast as I could."

Christina put her hand to her mouth and Rey took her other hand into his.

"A few blocks later, I took a corner too fast for that car. I T-boned a pickup truck so I got out and ran. The police searched the area all night and they eventually caught all three of us. I told them I didn't know that the guys were going to shoot. I thought we were going to get into a fistfight, but they didn't believe me."

David stood up and moved to the porch railing. He looked out over the street for a second and then turned back to Rey and Christina.

"One of the guys in the backseat took a plea deal and ratted on me and the shooter. They charged me with three counts of accessory to murder and sentenced me to thirty years in the penitentiary. I get my first chance for parole after fifteen years, which is coming up soon. I got a pretty raw deal for driving some people around in a car, if you ask me."

"That's horrible," Christina whispered to Rey, but loud enough for David to hear.

David snapped his attention toward Christina. "What's horrible?"

"Those three men are dead over a drug deal."

"I just helped take three more losers off the street, just like the state did when they locked me and my boys up. We were all just a bunch of losers."

Rey noticed the pained look on Christina's face, so he asked, "That seems like a real negative way to describe yourself. Do you really think you were just a big loser?"

"If you lived my life story, wouldn't you?"

For the first time since he moved in, Rey felt sorry for David.

"What about the assault charge against a minor?" Christina asked.

"What about it?"

"I'd like to hear about what happened," she said.

"I don't want to talk about it."

"You told us about the murder charge, but you can't tell us about the assault?"

"I said, I don't want to talk about it!" he barked.

Silence overcame the front porch. Even the crickets in the yard seemed louder.

Rey attempted to break the tension. "Hey, it's getting late so let's head back inside."

Christina was already in bed when Rey came into the room. He quietly pulled back the comforter and climbed into bed. He stared into the darkness until he was startled by a voice.

"Pretty wild story, eh?" Christina said.

"I thought you were asleep," Rey replied.

"I keep thinking about David's story."

"Me too. It was disturbing to hear, but I was sorta glad to learn that he was the driver and not the shooter. That would be really disturbing."

Christina did not respond.

After thirty seconds of silence, Rey asked, "what did you think?"

"The disturbing part for me is that someone responsible for three murders was sitting on our front porch telling us he got a raw deal. Plus, he won't talk about the assault charge against a minor."

"Yeah, that's pretty messed up."

"I wonder if it's because we have two young kids and he doesn't want us to know he's a danger to them."

Rey turned his attention back to the blackness of the ceiling. Neither said another word that night.

CHAPTER TWENTY-EIGHT

The reunion with Christina and the kids was half over. They planned to go back to San Antonio in three days, so Rey was trying to get all his work done early so he could spend the afternoon with his family, a luxury he never had as a CO.

Rey was about to shut down his laptop when an urgent email came through. It was from Deputy Director Scalise.

Did you read the incident report?

Rey hadn't checked since he first logged on, so he quickly read it. He couldn't believe his eyes. One of the RIHARP inmates tried to escape and the TDCJ host had to chase him down in the suburban neighborhood. The assistant controller at TDCJ found the inmate hiding under a boat in a neighbor's yard two blocks away and activated Sure Cuffs. It worked, but not before the homeowners called the police. The Austin police now had several questions for TDCJ about the RIHARP program and they wanted answers immediately.

Rey responded to his boss that he read the report. A new email emerged in his inbox a minute later. Mr. Scalise wanted Rey to interview the TDCJ employee and provide a complete report before nine o'clock tomorrow morning.

"Tomorrow?" Rey asked aloud. "That's going to take all day."

He moved to the end of the couch and contacted the assistant controller on a Zoom video call. For the next two hours, he interviewed the TDCJ employee and his wife. He gathered his notes and took a break for dinner. As soon as he finished eating, Rey started on his multi-page report.

Christina finished cleaning up in the kitchen and called for the kids to get ready for their showers. She disappeared down the hall into Noah's room so she could help him get ready for his shower.

David went into his room and shut the door. Five minutes later he walked into the family room. "Excuse me, Rey, I need some air. Can we go outside for a little bit?"

Rey didn't even look up from his screen. "Not right now. I've got to get this done. Maybe later."

David went back to his room and shut his door again, but this time he only stayed for two minutes before he reappeared in the family room.

Rey stopped typing and looked up at David. "I said I was terribly busy, David. What is it?"

"Why can't we go outside now? I don't ask very often anymore. I need some air now."

"I heard you the first time, but you aren't listening to me. I said I need to get this done first and then we can go outside, but if you keep interrupting me, we may not be able to go outside tonight."

"What?" David roared.

Rey flinched at the abrupt reply. In a firm voice, he responded, "I said you need to let me finish or we won't be able to go out tonight."

Both men locked their narrowing eyes on each other.

I've seen those eyes before as a CO. He's trying to read me. He's testing me to see how far he can push his boundaries. Stand firm.

David turned around and took two steps toward his room and then bolted for the front door. He was out the door before Rey was off the couch, but Rey was faster. David jumped down the stairs and landed the bottom when Rey arrived on the front porch.

"Get back inside now, David."

"I'm tired of you telling me no. I'm not going back in."

Rey kept his eyes on David as he slowly walked down the stairs. He stopped a few yards from David on the sidewalk. "You need to get back inside right now or I'm going to activate Sure Cuffs."

"Whatever," David snickered and turned away from the house.

Rey pulled his phone out of his pocket, opened the Sure Cuffs app and hit Activate.

David took one step and then straightened up and stopped at the end of the sidewalk. Rey put the phone back in his pocket. He exhaled and approached David.

"I'm sorry, but you made me—"

David hopped on both feet toward Rey and swung at him with his right hand. Rey wasn't expecting David to be able to move so he didn't have his hands up to protect himself. The punch first connected with Rey's shoulder and careened off to connect just above his ear.

Rey winced at the pain and took a step back. He saw David's left arm snug at his side, but his right arm was not secure at all. David crouched and cocked his right arm for another punch. Rey was ready this time and dodged the blow. He took a step to his right and grabbed David behind the neck. He took the wobbly inmate down into the grass in one motion.

David landed face down in the turf. Rey knelt in the middle of David's back. His knee moved a few inches every time David yelled into the freshly cut lawn. David eventually turned his head to catch his breath and attempted to grab at Rey with this right arm. Rey snatched his free arm and secured it behind David's back like he'd done hundreds of times before as a corrections officer.

Rey pushed David's arm up his back and yelled, "Stop resisting!"

Christina heard the commotion and appeared on the porch. "Rey!" she screamed.

Rey turned and yelled, "go get my cuffs. They're in the closet on top of the safe."

She arrived a minute later with the handcuffs and passed them to Rey. He slid them over David's right wrist and then tried to pull his left wrist behind his back. It wouldn't budge. Rey tried again.

"It's attached to my hip, it ain't going nowhere," David shouted into the grass.

Rey looked over to Christina again. She was standing with one hand over her mouth and the other hand over her stomach. Rey could see her shaking.

"Christina, I need you to deactivate Sure Cuffs so I can get David's other wrist in cuffs. Can you do that?"

Christina nodded and pulled the phone from her back pocket. Five seconds later, Rey could feel David's left arm pull away from his body. He quickly pulled it behind his back and secured him in the traditional hand cuffs. Rey stood up and went over to Christina.

"What happened?" Christina's voice cracked as she touched the scratch above Rey's ear.

Rey turned to David still laying in the prone position with his arms behind his back.

"He wanted to go outside and I said no because I was busy writing my report that's due tomorrow, so he just bolted outside. I chased after him and activated Sure Cuffs, but they didn't work. At least not completely. He got me with one punch and then I was able to subdue him. That's when you came out."

"So, the Sure Cuffs doesn't work?"

Rey turned to face Christina. He could tell by her tone that a failure was a potential deal breaker for her, and he needed to provide a suitable response.

He was saved by his phone when it rang in his hand. Rey quickly answered.

"This is Brian from Sectronix we received a notification of a Sure Cuffs activation. To whom am I speaking?"

"This is Rey Mendoza."

"Thank you, Mr. Mendoza. I need to confirm your identity. What is your password?"

Rey walked to the end of the sidewalk and shared his passwords.

"Mr. Mendoza, is everyone at your residence okay? Do I need to send the police or an ambulance?

Rey carefully considered the question as a range of potential outcomes ran through his head. If he requested the police, David would likely be sent back to Huntsville making it possible for Christina and the kids to move back in. Then RIHARP would surely be terminated and never see the light of day again. On the other hand, if Rey declined the police, he could manage this malfunction directly with John Nickerson to preserve RIHARP, but risk keeping his family away longer. This was exactly the type of decision he hoped he'd never have to make.

"Mr. Mendoza, should I send the police or an ambulance?"

What would Scalise say if he knew what happened?

"I'm not getting a reply from the resident, so I'm going to dispatch both the police and ambulance."

"No, no! Don't send either. Everyone is fine here. Just assessing the situation after an accidental activation of Sure Cuffs."

"So it was an accidental activation?"

"Yes, I was showing my wife how the app worked, and I accidently hit activate. Everything is fine now."

Rey clicked the end call button and then watched Christina disappear into the house. Rey helped David up by the back of his collar and guided him into the house. Rey pushed David down on the bed and showed him the key to the handcuffs.

"Are you going to give me any more problems tonight?"

David stared at Rey without responding.

"If you do, I'll cuff you again and drive you all the way back to Huntsville myself. Your time outside will be over. You hear me?"

David nodded.

Rey waited until David made eye contact and once he was satisfied David's outburst was over, he removed the cuffs. Rey left the room and shut the door behind him.

Fixing the malfunction was Rey's highest priority. He pulled out his phone and called John.

"Hi, John, sorry for calling so late but I need you to come to my house right away."

"Why? What happened?"

"We had a major Sure Cuffs malfunction tonight and we need to address it immediately."

"What kind of malfunction?"

"I'll tell you more when you get here."

Rey looked down the hall and saw Christina pacing in the master bedroom.

"Bring all your supplies to analyze and fix Sure Cuffs in an inmate and come as soon as possible. Hurry!"

CHAPTER TWENTY-NINE

Forty minutes later, Rey met John as soon as he pulled into the driveway.

"I came as fast as I could. What's going on?"

"I'm going to take you inside to see my RIHARP inmate. We had a Sure Cuffs malfunction earlier tonight. I was able to subdue him thanks to my CO training, but it really scared my wife."

"Oh, no. What happened?"

"Do you have everything you need to analyze Sure Cuffs?" Rey asked.

"Yeah, everything is in the back. I have the RFID reader which will tell me if every microchip is sending and receiving a signal. I also have a new set of Sure Cuffs transmitters if we need them."

Next, Rey shared all the details of the confrontation with David. John asked several follow up questions and nodded in silence to each response.

"Okay, I'm ready to see him now," John said.

Everyone was in their bedroom with the doors shut. They found David lying on his bed watching TV.

"John, this is David. He's our RIHARP guest."

David kept his eyes on John as he sat up.

"David, this is John. He's the inventor and owner of Sure

Cuffs. He's going to evaluate why they malfunctioned tonight. Do you have a problem with that?"

David's eyes widened when John set down two bags. "I guess I don't really have a choice, do I?"

Rey moved closer to David. He stared at him until David's impish grin vanished. Once Rey was sure he had David's full attention, he responded in a slow, measured voice. "Yes, you have a choice. You can refuse and serve the remainder of your sentence in Huntsville or you can cooperate with the opportunity to remain here under the RIHARP program."

David glared at Rey but didn't respond.

"So is that a yes, you'll cooperate or a no, you want to go back to your cell in Huntsville?"

"Yes, I'll cooperate," David huffed like a frustrated teenager.

"Good," Rey replied with a forced smile.

John removed the RFID reader from his bag. "David, please stand up."

He held the reader over David's left shoulder and moved it all the way down to his ankle. John watched his smart phone for the readings. He repeated the process on David's right side three times.

John placed his RFID reader back in his bag. "The chips in his right wrist and arm malfunctioned."

"Why? How?" Rey asked.

"I don't know yet, but I'll have to remove the existing chips and replace them with new chips."

"Can you do that now?" Rey asked.

"Yes, it doesn't take too long. It'll take me about five minutes to get the chips ready to insert."

John turned to David.

"You okay with that?"

"It'd be my pleasure." David responded with a sarcastic grin.

After John implanted and tested the new microchips, they returned to his SUV. Rey stopped John before he got in.

"John, this can't happen to a citizen when we roll RIHARP out to the general public. Sure Cuffs can't malfunction for them. Ever. It needs to be one hundred percent effective. How do we do that?"

"I guess we could scan every inmate with the RFID reader when the inmate is dropped off at their host's house like we do in prison after we embed the chips."

Rey returned a weak nod. Then an idea struck. "Couldn't we just have the new hosts activate Sure Cuffs to verify it works? It would give them much needed practice with the app plus more confidence that Sure Cuffs can protect them and their families?"

John shifted his weight and furrowed his brow. "Yeah, it's possible, but it's not very comfortable for the inmate."

"I understand, but if the inmate knew Sure Cuffs was going to be activated, maybe it wouldn't be so bad. I'm thinking it would be best to do both steps until we are Sure Cuffs is one-hundred percent effective. I'm going to write up a RFID reader test and Sure Cuffs activation test by the hosts during all transfer meetings into the operations manual."

Christina was asleep when Rey arrived in bed after midnight. He was used to physical confrontations with inmates, but this was the first time she'd witnessed an inmate outburst that required him to be physically detained. Rey remembered his first take down at the Torres Unit. His heart rate was so high that he couldn't sleep after that shift.

He felt Christina toss and turn all night. All Rey could do was pray.

The next day, Christina stopped Rey when he returned home from work. "I'm going to take the kids back to San Antonio tonight. I know I said we'd stay longer, but I just can't. I can't do this."

"Please don't go. Sure Cuffs is fixed."

"I'm sorry. We can't stay."

Rey felt like his head slipped below the surface of a cold lake. He saw himself sinking but couldn't do anything to stop it.

"We didn't get a chance to talk about the job offer yet."

"I don't think it needs much discussion. We both know what I need to do."

Rey's heart sank when the door closed behind Christina and the kids.

For the next two weeks, the Project Second Chance team worked hard to add the new procedure to Sure Cuffs. They added the step for new hosts to test Sure Cuffs on the arriving inmates and received final approval from Deputy Director Scalise.

That year, the first day in July was on a Tuesday, so it was also the second monthly RIHARP meeting with all the hosts. Similar to the last meeting, incident reports were read, and discussion of the attempted escape lasted nearly an hour. Several suggestions were put forward on how to mitigate another inmate escape attempt. Sure Cuffs was currently designed to stop and subdue an inmate. It was exclusively up to the hosts to prevent an escape.

As the deadline neared for the hosts to pick up their inmates from the conference room, discussion of the upcoming holiday weekend plans broke out in the room.

One host member said they were camping in Hill Country and another was going to a music festival.

"Who is going to watch your inmate?" Rey inquired.

Answers of brother, neighbor and cousin were returned by various hosts. They were all provided with the Sure Cuffs app and instructed how to use it.

Rey nodded in approval. "Interesting."

"What are you doing for the fourth?" Carrie asked Rey.

"I'm staying home with my inmate. My wife and her parents are taking the kids to the Schlitterbahn Waterpark. They'll stay a couple nights and watch the fireworks there."

"Oh, that sounds fun. Why don't you go too?"

Rey dropped his head and exhaled. He looked up again at

Carrie. "Maybe in the future, but not right now. I don't have anyone else who can watch my inmate."

"Sorry. I'd watch him if I was going to be in town. It's like you are the one in prison now, not him."

Rey opened his mouth, but no sound emerged. He nodded and turned to the rest of the team. "Y'all did a great job this week. We've made several improvements to RIHARP thanks to you."

Everyone on the team nodded. A few high fives were exchanged.

"Enjoy your long weekend. I'll see you on Monday."

Christina was beaming when she reached Rey on FaceTime Sunday night. Despite their current exhaustion, the kids had non-stop fun going down the water slides all day, she reported. "I haven't seen them have that much fun in a while."

"I'm grateful your parents were able to treat the kids to such a fun time. It has been a long time since we've been able to spoil them."

"We'll be able to do more once the school year starts and I bring in a paycheck again."

"I know. I just wish it didn't have to be this way," Rey whispered.

"Me either. We'll be together under one roof again sometime soon. Keep praying and don't lose hope."

Rey did just that and after three weeks of routine days at the office and construction after work, he was getting closer to completion of the home remodel project. He was also getting closer to getting his family back.

One morning, Rey woke up to the sound of running water. He turned over in his bed and put the pillow over his head.

"How long of a shower is he going to take?"

Rey marched out of his room toward the hallway bathroom. He was ready to pound on the door to tell David to speed up his hygiene process.

He nearly slipped and fell in the hall. Rey looked down at the pool of water forming on the wood floors in the hallway.

"Leak!" he cried.

Rey splashed through the puddles until he reached the bathroom. He looked inside and saw a geyser erupting from the new sink he installed earlier in the week.

At the same time Rey arrived on the scene, David opened his door. "What's going on?"

"I need to find the shut off valve!" Rey shouted as he battled the spray of water pummeling his chest.

Rey dropped to his knees below the pedestal sink and turned both valves. The rush of water stopped. He turned and fell back against the wall. Rey sat with water dripping from his ears, nose and chin as he assessed the situation.

"I must not have installed the new faucet correctly. I have to start all over now."

David took a big step over the water in the hallway to the small island formed on the doorway. "I can help you if you need it," he offered.

"Thanks. We better get this water cleared up before the floors warp."

David gathered towels from the linen closet, and together they mopped and wrung towels for the next two hours. David suggested they set up a fan in the hallway to dry the places they couldn't mop.

That afternoon, Rey called Christina. He told her about the disaster in the bathroom.

"Could you have your parents watch the kids for a few days? I need to run out to get new supplies so I can fix this bathroom and potentially even the hallway. Can you hang out here for a few days and help me with this?

Christina agreed and two days later, she arrived, turning the negative event into a positive one for Rey.

CHAPTER THIRTY

Christina stayed in the house to watch David while Rey went back and forth to the hardware store to purchase the materials needed to fix the bathroom and hall floor. When Rey was out, Christina spent her time on her phone, not only for news and entertainment, but for quick access to the Sure Cuffs app. She didn't talk to David when he occasionally emerged from his room to get a snack.

Christina helped Rey with the bathroom repairs and after two days of manual labor, she fell asleep minutes after hitting the pillow on her last night in Austin.

But some hours after falling asleep, she heard the floor creak in the hallway and her eyes shot open. She looked at the clock and saw it was one thirty in the morning. Rey dozed beside her.

She stretched her neck to peer into the hallway illuminated by a nightlight but didn't see any movement and assumed she must be imagining noises. Content it was just her overanxious imagination, she laid her head back down after confirming the hallway was quiet. Despite her best efforts to fall back asleep, her mind was racing with possibilities.

Could that have been David?

A sour feeling exploded in her gut and she opened her eyes again.

A new noise came from the hallway and this time Christina sat up in bed. She held her breath so she could hear the faintest sounds. Slow, quiet steps were getting a little louder with each new step toward their bedroom. It was like a leopard plotting an opportune time to spring on its prey. A shadow appeared on the wall once the figure passed the nightlight that confirmed Christina's worst fear. A person was slinking toward her bedroom.

Christina turned and shook Rey.

"What is it?"

"Somebody's coming into our room."

CHAPTER THIRTY-ONE

Rey sprang up in bed and fixed his gaze on the shadow of a man only steps from their doorway. He squinted and angled his head to see if it was David, but the shadow was too distorted on the wall to confirm whether it was him. He considered diving toward his gun safe in the closet, but instead chose to stop the man before he could get into the room. The man stopped just outside the bedroom doorway as Rey charged him. Rey lowered his head and tackled the man like his high school football coach taught him sixteen years earlier. The men slammed into the moist wooden floor. A second later, Rey heard shouts coming from a familiar voice.

"It's me, man. It's David. It's just me."

Rey jumped up and shouted back, "What are you doing?"

David sat up and leaned on one arm, "I couldn't sleep so I wanted to see if either of you was awake so I could go outside."

"You know you're not supposed to be down here," Rey roared. "It's in the middle of the night. What are you thinking?"

David didn't answer.

"Go back to your room and we'll deal with this tomorrow."

"I was just checking to see if anyone was awake. I thought I heard someone up."

"I said we'll talk about this in the morning."

Rey returned to the bedroom and found Christina standing next to the bed clutching her pillow. Rey turned on the lamp on his nightstand and saw the evidence of tears running down her face.

"What's going on?"

"It was David. He said he wanted to go outside and thought we were awake. He's back in his room now."

"I'm not going to be able to go back to sleep now. There must be a better way to host an inmate. This isn't working."

Rey twisted his wedding ring several rotations and then rubbed the back of his neck. He couldn't present any type of defense for the danger she felt. Plus, she was right. This isn't working and he needed to find a better way.

"I'm sorry. I'll stay up so you can go back to sleep. I'll read in the chair."

Christina stared at him. Rey guessed she was questioning whether to leave now or considering the benefit of more sleep before driving back to San Antonio.

She laid back down in bed and pulled up the sheets.

Rey couldn't tell if she fell asleep but was happy that she was at least trying. She worked hard the last two days and needed to get some rest before resuming her role as the single parent with Noah and Maddie again.

He watched her breathe and thought hard about solutions.

Dozens of options ran through his mind until a sliver of sun began to peek through the window.

Christina stirred and then got up. A few minutes later, she said she was ready to go.

"Are you sure? It's still so early."

Christina answered with a look. Rey knew it was time to let her go.

She left without a hug or kiss and Rey didn't even protest. Last night was the low point. It was worse than he thought it ever could be since they moved out.

Rey needed a better solution to hosting an inmate.

His family depended on it.

The click of the latch bolt sliding into place after Christina left still echoed in Rey's mind. He moved into the family room and stared at the black TV screen.

After a deep sigh, he looked to Heaven and then let his head flop forward.

How do I fix this?

Rey turned on the TV to find quick a distraction. He watched the familiar morning news crew on the screen but didn't really see anything. A minute later, he wiped away two rogue tears before they reached his cheek.

Rey opened his laptop and started his own incident report. He classified the confrontation with his RIHARP inmate as a "major incident." He knew it could add a stain to RIHARP and put the program in jeopardy, but he needed to get their attention. He couldn't incorporate the reforms and improvements to inmate conditions he wanted with RIHARP in its current form. RIHARP had to make the hosts feel safe and secure so they would be willing to give inmates a second chance on the other side of prison bars. Everything was riding on fixing this problem.

Once the report was complete, Rey followed protocol and submitted the report. He also sent a copy directly to John at Sectronix, so he'd see it right away.

Forty minutes later Rey's phone rang.

"I'm sorry, Rey," John said. "I hate that you're having a problem with your inmate."

"We need to fix this as soon as possible. This is a deal breaker for Sure Cuffs."

The phone went silent.

"Hello? John, are you still there?"

"Let me call you back."

Rey heard a click on the other end. He looked at his phone as if it just said something offensive. A second later he slowly pressed the end call button.

Several emails and two conference calls later, Rey saw that he missed five calls from John in the last two hours. He looked to see if he left a voicemail, but there were no notifications. He started to call John back when he saw John was calling him. Rey clicked over to John.

"I think I have a solution!" John was talking faster and louder than normal.

Rey didn't even get a moment to respond.

"One of the suggestions from the last monthly review really stuck with me," he continued, "so I've been working on it behind the scenes. We need to add GPS to Sure Cuffs."

"Okay. How's that going to work?"

"I talked to my engineering team and they said we can program the transmitters to activate Sure Cuffs if they cross a virtual boundary using GPS. It's accurate within three feet and can even detect elevation changes, so we can erect a virtual fence for the host families."

Rey pursed his lips and nodded. "Would it be accurate enough to allow an inmate to stay home unsupervised so I could run errands and come back to the office?"

"I'd want to test it further, but yeah. If an inmate crosses a GPS boundary, Sure Cuffs will automatically activate, and we'll get a notification. We'll be on the scene before they know what hit them."

"That's sounds like a great solution, John. Why didn't we add this in the first place?"

John sighed. "I'm embarrassed that I didn't think of it sooner. Sometimes it takes an event like this to spur the innovation that will improve the product for everyone else. I can't express how sorry I am that this happened to your family."

"It's okay. How soon can we get GPS added to Sure Cuffs?"

"It's going to take some time to generate all the code, so I'll have to send over a new work order."

"Send it over as soon as possible and I'll push for approval as fast as I can."

Rey felt a sensation engulf his body that has eluded him in recent months. It was hope.

CHAPTER THIRTY-TWO

John sent over the new work order the next day. Rey submitted it that same day but was not able to get a quick approval that week like he expected.

Rey's phone rang and he saw it was his boss. He was ready to defend his work request on the GPS. He wasn't expecting to hear Deputy Director Scalise's first question.

"How soon will RIHARP be ready to launch to the general public?"

Rey was ready to defend the request for GPS and the hefty price tag, so it took him a few extra seconds to respond.

"Ready for the general public?"

"Yeah, I've got finance crawling all over me about IT projects that are delayed, over budget or both."

"I still don't understand, sir."

Deputy Director Scalise paused and exhaled loudly into the phone. "RIHARP needs to be approved by the senior board of directors in six months or it's dead."

"What? It was originally twelve months!" Rey cried into the phone.

"No project is given an open calendar and blank checks, especially in IT. As much as I'm rooting for RIHARP, this department has a whole range of projects that must be completed. The time is now for RIHARP, so we need to move it from concept to active program in six months. Not a day longer."

Rey was silent on his end.

"I'm counting on you, Rey. Can we do it?"

"Yes," Rey whispered.

A list of all the additional work and improvements that had to be done in order to present RIHARP to the board was growing in Rey's head. His chest tightened and he started to breathe faster. A warm ball of nerves expanded in his stomach making Rey slightly nauseated.

How am I going to get RIHARP ready in six months?

"Good," Mr. Scalise continued. "I also received this request for eight thousand dollars to add GPS to Sure Cuffs. What's this about?"

Rey did not respond.

"If this is a bad time, I can call back later."

Rey took a deep breath and focused on the current issue. "No, now is fine. Did you read my incident report from last week?" Rey asked.

"I believe I did, but please refresh my memory."

Rey explained what happened with David in his hallway the previous week and the conversation with John the next day.

"GPS will solve a lot of the problems, so I asked John to send in the new work order."

"That's a lot of money. Is GPS a necessity for RIHARP?"

To release his building frustration, Rey wanted to yell, *Yes, GPS is an absolute necessity for the success of RIHARP. How can you not see that? Are you just worried about the money?* But he didn't.

Instead, he pressed the speaker button and placed his phone on the table. After taking a deep breath, he started. "I have a long list of reasons why GPS is needed for RIHARP. GPS can act as a virtual fence around a host property or even designated areas within a home. It can allow future hosts to restrict certain areas from inmate access. This would be invaluable to a future host.

Plus, what happens if an inmate walks out of the house in the middle of the night when nobody is awake? If nobody knows the inmate is missing, they can't activate Sure Cuffs until he's long gone. Another RIHARP inmate on the loose would surely kill this program, not to mention be a black eye for all TDCJ."

Rey was nearly out of breath. He inhaled and continued.

"How many times have you seen me in the office since my inmate arrived? I believe you could count them on one hand over the past two months."

"Yes, but the directors agreed to allow hosts to work from home during the beta program. We need to have constant supervision of the inmates until we are sure the policies, procedures and technology works as planned," Deputy Director Scalise reminded Rey.

"I understand and that was a very generous decision from the directors, but how many future hosts are going to have that option?"

Mr. Scalise did not respond.

"We need to make citizen hosts feel as safe, secure, and free as possible if we want RIHARP to be a success. I feel like I traded places with my inmate since I don't have anyone else to watch him. Plus, if we ever—"

"Okay, okay, Rey. I get it. We need GPS," Mr. Scalise interrupted. "The trouble is, we don't have the money in our budget for GPS. We'll need to cut back from somewhere else or I should say, you need to cut back on something. Are you willing to find me the money in your budget?"

"I am."

"Okay, I'm going to hold you to it. I'll sign the work order, but that's it for additions to RIHARP. It will need to work with what you've got."

"Yes, sir," Rey replied.

"Savings, Mr. Mendoza. I need to see how you're going to cover this in two days."

Mr. Scalise ended the call, but Rey kept the phone in his hand. He called John at Sectronix.

John answered, "Hey, Rey."

"Hey John. I have some good news and some bad news. I'll give you the good news first."

"Don't most people start with the bad news?"

"Not this time. The good news is that Mr. Scalise signed the work order to add the GPS."

"That's great news, but I'm afraid to hear the bad news."

"The bad news is that you need to do it in half the time, and I need to cut your monthly retainer by ten-percent for the next four months to cover the cost of the GPS."

"That's two thousand dollars a month!" John protested.

"I know. It wasn't an easy sell to the deputy director, but we need to look at the long game here. RIHARP and therefore Sure Cuffs won't fly with the public without GPS, but with GPS the program becomes more attractive. It will help Sure Cuffs move out of beta testing with a chance to expand the program across the whole state of Texas. If even five percent of the prison population qualified for this program, it would be big for Sectronix."

"Okay, you're right. I'll figure out how to make it work, but why in half the time? What's the rush?"

Rey considered telling John about his new ultimatum to finish in six months, but choose to save him from the added stress that he was sure to endure. Instead, he gave him the one answer that would make John want to fix it faster.

"RIHARP hosts aren't safe without it."

CHAPTER THIRTY-THREE

John came through as promised. He cut the development time in half, but it still took a week to test GPS with all the inmates in the RIHARP program. It worked to perfection with the eleven other hosts. Rey and David were the last to be tested.

John and his team set the coordinates based on the boundaries Rey established for David. He would have access to everywhere in the house, but not past his bathroom in the hallway. All the other bedrooms were off limits. David was also given access to the front porch, but nothing beyond the front steps.

John activated the GPS and announced, "It's ready to test on David."

Rey called David into the hallway. John and Rey stayed next to David to catch him if he fell.

"David, go ahead and walk past the bathroom." John ordered.

David took a step past the bathroom and nothing happened.

"Take another step."

David took another step. Once again, Sure Cuffs did not activate. Rey exhaled loudly and shook his head. "It doesn't work."

"Just start walking, David. All the way back to the master bedroom," John instructed.

David took two more steps until he was within a step or two of Noah's room. This time David stiffened, and his arms and legs locked together at his side. He looked like the wobbly soldier Rey was expecting.

"It works!" Rey rejoiced.

He gently tugged on David's arms and legs to ensure they were both snug next to his body. Once he was satisfied, he deactivated Sure Cuffs on his phone. He thanked David for his cooperation and sent him to the kitchen to enjoy the donuts John brought.

"It works," Rey told John, "but that's a little too close to Noah's room."

"That's an easy fix. GPS is accurate up to one meter so now that we've calibrated it in your house, we can adjust the coordinates, so his boundary is another step or two back from here."

"Perfect. Do you think I can go to work in the office now instead of working from home every day?"

John pursed his lips and paused before responding. "We are twelve for twelve on RIHARP inmates with the GPS test, so the technology works. At some point, you just have to have faith that David won't attempt to abuse his freedom and that Sure Cuffs will work if he does."

Rey smiled. "Amen to that."

After John left, Rey went into his closet to ensure he had clean clothes for the office. It had been so long since he'd had to go into the office that he still had work clothes in his hamper. He danced back to the washer with his dirty clothes.

The addition of GPS provided a major boost to the feasibility of RIHARP and a big step to approval in six months. Rey pondered his life as he poured the cup of blue detergent into the washing machine.

Could this be a turning point to my run of bad luck?

CHAPTER THIRTY-FOUR

Rey considered calling Christina to tell her the news. He planned to pound out a few more emails before he made the call. His phone rang on the table next to his laptop. It was Christina.

"Are you reading my mind? I was just about to call you."

"I'm taking Noah to urgent care."

"What? What happened?"

"I took him to get some shoes that fit, and a new smoke shop opened up next door to the shoe store. When we walked out of the shoe store, several people were smoking out front. I told Noah to hold his breath while I rushed him past the people, but I guess he inhaled some smoke. He's wheezing and has shortness of breath so I'm going to take him in."

"Text me as soon as you get him checked in."

"You don't need to come down. I've got this. I just wanted you to know about Noah."

"I can be there in less than two hours."

Rey hung up the phone and rushed to his room and changed. He prayed that the GPS worked because he was going to leave David home alone for the first time.

He stopped by David's room before he left. "David, I'm going to leave you home alone. My son is sick, so I need to go see how he is doing. The GPS is on so don't go beyond the boundaries. Once Sure Cuffs is activated, you'll be stuck for a long time before someone arrives."

"I hope your son is okay. Don't worry about me. I'll be here when you get back."

The sincerity in David's response caused Rey to pause. "Thank you."

"No problem. Have a safe trip."

Rey looked at his phone. "Ten minutes. I've got to get going."

He scrambled to his truck. Before he could pull off his street, his phone rang.

"Rey, you don't need to come down here. They're giving Noah oxygen and he's almost back to normal. He's going to be okay."

"I'm already in my truck. I can be there in ninety minutes."

After a short pause, Christina replied, "I'd prefer you didn't drive all the way down here. I just want to get Noah back home and let him rest. Can we talk later about the next time you'll drive down here?"

Rey exhaled loudly into the phone. He wanted to be sure Christina heard it. "Okay. Tell Noah and Maddie I love them."

"I will."

Rey pulled over and put his truck in park. He stared out the window at the passing cars. Christina didn't need him like she used to. She was drifting away.

Rey never felt so alone.

CHAPTER THIRTY-FIVE

For the next two weeks, Rey worked a shortened schedule at the office so he could check in with David at random times. Once Rey was convinced that David wasn't going to test the GPS boundaries, he began to work full days at the office. During his first week at a full schedule, it was time for the monthly RIHARP review meeting. He brought David to the TDCJ office like before, but this time he had to temporarily disable the GPS before leaving so David didn't collapse in a heap in his front lawn.

The meeting started and the other TDCJ hosts shared stories of their interactions with their inmates. Rey smiled as host after host provided more evidence that RIHARP was working as well as expected. Tim from IT support services was next to share his story, but he stared silently at his notepad sitting at a slight angle on the table.

"Tim, can you share how your last month went with your RIHARP inmate."

Tim looked up and his lips were quivering. "He attacked my son."

Nobody took a breath. All eyes snapped their gaze to Tim and not a single mouth was closed. Several hosts collectively cried out, "What?"

"He—. My boy was—" Tim looked back down at his notepad.

"Take your time. We're in no hurry," Rey comforted him.

He looked up at the group and continued. "My boy and inmate have been trading barbs since he first arrived. It was all in fun. My son is sixteen and our inmate is only ten years older, so I actually thought they were forming a friendship, but then he just snapped."

Tears welled up in Tim's narrow eyes. "It all happened so fast. He attacked my son faster than a rattlesnake strike and busted my son's nose with one punch. He got in a few more before I could activate Sure Cuffs."

Audible gasps came from the other hosts.

"My son had to stay in the hospital for a night with a concussion."

Tim's voice cracked and the tears he'd been holding back could no longer be contained. Several hosts got up and moved next to Tim. He waved them off as they got near him. "I'm okay, I'm okay."

Rey waited until everyone got back to their seats. "I'm so sorry, Tim."

Tim nodded.

"Did Sure Cuffs work when you hit the activate button?"

Tim shook his head, "I don't know. It all happened so fast. I'm pretty sure it worked, but it was too late. My son's nose was broken before I even picked up my phone. It was so fast."

Deputy Director Scalise pulled Rey aside after they left the conference room. "I need you to document everything about this incident by first thing tomorrow. This is not a good sign for RIHARP."

Rey considered mounting a protest in defense of RIHARP but read the deputy director's face and concluded now was a bad time.

"I'm surprised we didn't hear about this from the incident reports."

"I did." Deputy Director Scalise replied.

"How come I didn't get it?"

"It was sent directly to legal. A TDCJ inmate assaulted a minor and it required a hospital stay. Waiver or no waiver, this is going to cost TDCJ and it should."

Rey nodded.

"I'm meeting with legal on Thursday afternoon, so that gives you less than forty-eight hours to get me the completed incident report."

Rey looked at his phone. It was already three o'clock so he would have homework that night.

During the drive home, Rey pictured the horror Tim's family must have gone through to have their son attacked in their own home. He looked in the rear-view mirror at David in the back seat of his truck. He reminded Rey of a little boy as he looked out the window at the passing world. Rey couldn't picture David turning on him, but Tim probably thought the same thing about his inmate. After all this time, Rey still didn't know David very well and that needed to change.

Rey met John from Sectronix in the lobby the next morning and shared the news of the attack.

"John, you'll see the incident report in a couple of days. An inmate attacked the teenage son of one of our RIHARP hosts. He said it happened so fast, he couldn't get his phone out to activate Sure Cuffs before his son suffered a broken nose and a concussion."

"Oh, my gosh, that's horrible."

"What can we do to activate Sure Cuffs in a split second in the event a phone is not available or fast enough?"

John looked out the large bank of windows and pursed his lips. He nodded as he rubbed his goatee. "There may be a way."

Rey waited several seconds as John focused on the floor before he asked, "Can you do it?"

"Yeah, I think we can. We've been testing another way to activate Sure Cuffs that would be a lot faster. We could use sound."

"How would that work?"

"We'd give the hosts a safety word and then program it into Sure Cuffs as a verbal activation. We could also do a loud noise like a yell or bang on a table to activate it. I'm still working on a minimum decibel level to make sure it doesn't go off too easy for something like a dog bark or crying baby. I need to run more tests."

"That would be great. How long will it take?" Rey asked.

John shook his head. "We are already pretty close with this improvement, so probably four or five days."

"This should be our last improvement to RIHARP, so let's do it."

CHAPTER THIRTY-SIX

John turned to leave the lobby but stopped and turned back to Rey. "I can't do any more for free, so I'll have to charge you for this change."

"How much?"

"Since we are close, this will only be an extra three thousand dollars."

"What about investing in Sure Cuffs now so you can make it back when its approved at all the prisons across Texas?" Rey asked.

"I've been investing since this project started and I just spent my last reserves on coding the GPS project. This well is dry."

Rey thought about his conversation with Mr. Scalise. Somehow Rey managed to put himself in the worst possible scenario. He could risk upsetting his boss who had been very supportive of the Project Second Chance team and endure the repercussions of directly disobeying him. The other option was to risk the TDCJ board denying that RIHARP was ready for the public and allowing the project to be scrapped. Rey had so much invested in RIHARP and it went beyond his pride of doing a good job. The approval of RIHARP would avenge the injustice his father faced two decades earlier. And RIHARP was much more than an inmate reform program. It had become the lifeblood of Rey's deep-seated desire to change lives. The deputy director would sentence RIHARP to death if it couldn't prove its innocence or worth in six months. Unlike the RIHARP inmates, the RIHARP program wouldn't get a second chance. Rey was down to his final six months. His life purpose was at a crossroads.

"I appreciate all you've done so far, John. Go ahead and get started now and send me the work order for the three thousand. I'll get it approved."

John left the lobby and Rey went up to his desk. He needed to update the RIHARP policies and procedures with the new sound-activated option.

After a grueling week, Rey needed to get his mind off Sure Cuffs, RIHARP, and anything related to TDCJ. He chose to go climbing.

Saturday morning, he left David a note and headed to the Barton Creek greenbelt. It was his favorite place to climb and he'd been going there for years.

He'd just secured his harness and began to get a foothold when he heard a familiar voice. It was a fellow climber and a member of the University of Texas police force.

"It's Rey, right? You climbing alone?" The man asked.

"Yeah, I'm sorry to say I forgot your name," Rey admitted sheepishly.

"It's Josh. We climbed together a few times three or four years ago with the Travis County Climbers club."

The two men shook hands.

"Right, I thought you looked familiar. You still on the police force at UT?"

"Yep. Going on eight years now."

Rey gave his rope a tug to test the anchor bolt. "Great, wanna climb together?"

"You bet."

The two men started their climb and seventy-five minutes later they pulled themselves over the lip of the near vertical wall. They sat and slid back from the edge until they found another wall for back support. They cracked open their energy bars and sports drinks.

"You still a CO?" Josh asked.

"No, I took a job at the TDCJ main office in Austin about a year ago."

"Really? I remember you telling us about all the changes you planned to make with the inmates, stuff you learned while you were in Europe or somewhere. I kept hoping I'd hear some big change with the prisons in the news. You were so passionate, I thought you'd never do anything else."

Rey looked down and found a small pebble. He tossed it past his feet. "I've had a lot of changes in my life since then, but the passion to improve the lives of inmates is still strong. I'm just going to do it from a new role now."

"I hope so, man. I like catching the bad guys and putting them in jail, but I don't like what I hear about some of them when they get out. I'm not dealing with murderers or molesters on campus, but still, some of these guys come out worse criminals than when I arrested them."

"Yeah, that's what I'm hoping to change. Fewer repeat customers," Rey said with a half-smile.

"I love it. Look, Rey, I've got to get back for my afternoon shift, so I need to head down now."

"I need to get going too. I'll go down with you."

Rey pulled out slowly from the greenbelt parking lot. He kept replaying Josh's comments in his head.

Have I forgotten what Lars taught me since I took the TDCJ job? Am I doing anything to help David?

When Rey arrived home, he walked into the half-finished hallway bathroom. David had been jockeying sections of bare floor and emptying a bucket under the sink into the toilet because the sink was still broken.

He bent down and picked up his work belt. He tied it around his waist while looking into the mirror.

"David?"

"Yeah?" David answered from his room across the hall.

"Can you come in here? I need your help."

For the next week, Rey made progress on the home remodel and with David. He learned more about David's past.

Despite the early progress, it didn't last. Rey got frustrated with David's lack of mechanical aptitude. He was even less skilled than Rey, so Rey decided David was best assigned to demolition and clean up. David enjoyed only the former, so he was less helpful with each cleanup request. David also clammed up when asked about the assaulting a minor charge.

Frustration grew in Rey as he realized how much work he still had to do to get his family to move back. Both the house and David still weren't ready for them.

CHAPTER THIRTY-SEVEN

Rey grabbed his phone and plopped down on the family room couch. He scrolled through some social media sites with little interest until one post put a smile on his face.

His friend Captain Maxwell, the Air Force chaplain, had posted a picture of his family passing out food to people in a church parking lot. Rey sent a message to his old Air Force buddy asking him to meet sometime soon.

The next morning, Rey got a response and they coordinated schedules. Rey suggested they meet for lunch at Stubbs Bar-B-Q near downtown Austin on Saturday. He knew that was one Texas temptation that Captain Maxwell couldn't resist.

Saturday afternoon, they arrived at Stubbs and found a table in the corner. After the decadent barbeque dishes were delivered to their table, Captain Maxwell said grace. He turned to Rey, saying, "okay, enough small talk. I know you must have something on your mind to invite me to come all the way up here. So how are you really doing?"

Rey stabbed at his pulled pork. "Not good. Christina and the kids are living in our old house in San Antonio."

"Oh, I'm sorry. I didn't know you two were having problems. You should have contacted me sooner."

"It's not like that. Christina took the kids back to our house in San Antonio last year because we are remodeling our new home in Austin and the dust is horrible for Noah. We had to rush him to the ER a month after we moved in. Now, I have an inmate from Huntsville prison living in our house from that program at work. Christina doesn't feel safe living with him in the house, so she's not in a hurry to return and I don't know what to do."

"I know what you need to do."

Captain Maxwell stuck a forkful of sliced brisket in his mouth.

Rey leaned forward waiting for him to finish chewing and shed some light on his predicament.

He finished, wiped his mouth and pointed his fork at Rey. "Do everything in your power to get your wife and kids back in that house with you."

Rey sighed and then smiled. "I wish it was that easy. Christina's concerned about the safety of Noah and Maddie and I can't blame her."

His friend and mentor put his fork down and leaned toward Rey. "I'm afraid, you're afraid, we're all afraid of something. They key is to want something greater than your fear. Rey, you have that with your desire to save someone from a life of imprisonment. It's so powerful that you no longer fear."

"Yeah, but that's not what Christina wants. She is only trying to protect our kids. She's a great mother."

"Then you have to go further. Look for a new job or ship the guy back to Huntsville and request a new one. You have to do whatever it takes to get them back."

"I've already tried the new job route and I fought taking a prisoner as long as I could. My job depends on it and I finally feel I am in a position to do something major to improve conditions for the inmates. It's something that I've been driven to do for the last twenty years."

Captain Maxwell nodded. "I know."

"This new RIHARP program could be a real game changer for the entire prison system. I'd like to see more inmates in our system be one and done instead of repeat offenders. It's a big idea, but it's doable and I'd like to be part of it."

"I get it, but I can't help but think keeping a family together is equally as important. You know you can get involved in other things with an important purpose. Where are you going to church up here?"

Rey looked down at his food. Suddenly very interested in his pulled pork and side of beans.

"Rey Mendoza! You and Christina were very involved with your church down in San Antonio. I have someone I want you to meet. We're having coffee next Saturday and I want you to come with me. It's out past Barton Creek on highway two ninety. I'll text you the time and address."

"Who is it?"

Captain Maxwell leaned in and winked. "You'll see on Saturday."

CHAPTER THIRTY-EIGHT

Rey pulled out of his driveway Saturday morning and drove to Southwest Austin. His GPS guided him to a small building on the campus of a large church complex. The grounds were impeccable. Live oak trees stood guard around the parking lot and a large grassy expanse was beyond the rim of trees. Rey noticed the coffee shop sign and entered.

Once his eyes adjusted, he saw Captain Maxwell sitting at a table with another man. He looked to be a few years older than Rey, but with far more hipster fashion sense. He was wearing black skinny jeans with cowboy boots with an untucked long-sleeve button up shirt with silver beadwork. Rey stopped at the table and Captain Maxwell stood and gave him a hug.

He turned to the other man. "This is my friend Rey that I told you about. Rey, this is Pastor Scott. He's the executive pastor here at Hill Country Christian Church."

Pastor Scott shook Rey's hand. "Do you want anything from the coffee bar?"

"A black coffee would be great."

"Iced?"

"No, hot please."

Two minutes later, Pastor Scott arrived back with a steaming mug of coffee. He sat down at a square, four-person table across from Rey.

"Captain Maxwell tells me you're looking for a new church in Austin. He said you may want to get involved with something that can make a serious impact on the community. We have a lot of programs here that do that. What type of things are you interested in?"

"Well, Captain Maxwell is correct, but he did leave out one important piece of information. I have a plan to make an impact in the community at work, but I'd like to do more outside of work once my family moves back in. My wife and two kids are still in San Antonio now."

"Your family is living in San Antonio? I thought you lived here."

Rey told Pastor Scott the entire story. He started with accepting the job in Austin, remodeling the house, the RIHARP program and ended with his recent attempts to engage David in order to build trust so that Christina would feel comfortable moving back into their home.

After Rey finished his story, Pastor Scott exhaled and nodded. "I think you need to change your approach with David. You aren't giving him a reason to grow. You may be restricting his activities in the name of safety, but instead you are sending a message that you don't trust him. You need to make the first move to build trust. Let him experience the taste of feeling valued. It's something he may not have ever felt before."

Rey leaned back in his chair, "It sounds great coming from you, but how do I do it?"

Pastor Scott scanned the room as if he was looking for an answer on the walls or inspiration from the highly caffeinated shop patrons.

After a period of awkward silence, Captain Maxwell chimed in. "A puppy."

"A puppy?" Rey inquired.

"Yeah, a cute little puppy. You can pick one up at the local shelter."

Rey turned to Pastor Scott to gauge his reaction. He nodded, adding, "I've heard puppies melt even the most hardened men."

"Okay, if I get a puppy, how does that help me with David?"

Captain Maxwell and Pastor Scott looked at each other. Captain Maxwell said, "I'll tell him."

He smiled and began talking faster. "Get a puppy and put David in charge of it. Don't tell him what to do, just tell him it's his job to make sure the puppy is healthy, clean, fed, entertained and overall happy. Let him learn to fix his own mistakes. Let him form a bond and understand that he is responsible for this life. Then expand that sense of accountability and responsibility to other parts of his life. He needs to do all that if you ever want him to be successful outside of prison once he's served his time."

Rey looked back and forth at the two men. "Okay, how will I know when he's ready?"

"You'll just know," they answered in unison.

Rey stroked the day-old whiskers poking from his chin. "I think I get it."

That weekend Rey pondered all the ways he could empower David. He wasn't sure about a puppy just yet, so he floated his own ideas and shot them down all weekend.

Monday morning, Rey sent a one-sentence email to John at Sectronix: Please expand the GPS boundaries for David to the edge of my property.

CHAPTER THIRTY-NINE

The glow of morning sun filled the room as Rey reclined on his couch. He continued to think of ways to engage David and help him grow. A thought formed. Rey shot up from the couch and pumped both fists in the air.

"That's brilliant!" Rey yelled to the empty family room.

Christina had wanted Rey to fix the broken swing set in the backyard before she left. Rey could have David help him and then tell Christina to bring the kids up to test it out. A true win-win.

Rey looked out the kitchen window at the wobbly swing set. It was a like a newborn foal trying to steady itself. Rey was surprised it was still standing. After further analysis, Rey determined the tools and kind of assistance he would need to fix the swing set.

When Rey knocked on David's door, he answered, shirtless, within a few seconds. "Is the TV too loud?"

"No, I didn't even hear it. Can you help me fix the swing set in the backyard?"

A smile appeared on David's stubbly face. "Yeah, let me get a shirt on."

Rey grabbed his tools and walked through the back door with David following. David suddenly stopped.

"You coming?" Rey asked.

"Did you turn off the GPS? I don't want to do the virtual strait-jacket pose right now."

Rey laughed. "Oh, I forgot to tell you. I expanded the GPS to the edge of the property. You can go in the yard and patio anytime you want now."

"Really?" David asked as his voice cracked. "I don't have to ask anymore?"

"Nope. I trust ya."

David stood frozen near the back door. He took several slow steps forward to test if this expansion of his boundaries was indeed true.

"Come on. Let's fix this swing set for the kids."

A wide grin appeared on David's face and he jogged into the grassy yard.

Rey was greeted by a stiff breeze when he entered his back-yard. It was a welcome relief on this unusually warm and humid November day. After developing a brief plan of attack in his head, Rey approached the objective to fix the swing set with David in tow.

David steadied the frame from the ground while Rey climbed the ladder and tightened the rusty bolts. After repeating this process multiple times, the swing set began to take its intended shape. The swings blew back and forth as the sky darkened and gusts of wind increased their intensity. Rey tightened the final bolt and took several steps back. It was ready for Noah and Maddie.

"I can't wait to see Noah and Maddie on this. They're going to love it."

"Look!" David pointed to the sky.

Thick, dark cumulus clouds closed in on them from over the treetops. Sheets of rain were visible, and they appeared to be blocks away.

"That's pretty close. Let's grab the tools and head inside before it hits us."

A minute later, large drops started slowly and then the skies unleashed their fury with a full deluge of rain.

"Drop the tools and let's get inside."

They both scampered toward the house. Rey flinched, but did not break stride at a nearby lightning strike. A loud rumble of thunder followed seconds later. Rey turned around to verify David was following close behind and saw him lying on the ground.

Oh my gosh, did he get struck by lightning?

Rey returned to David where he was face down in the grass. Rey turned him over onto his back. David's eyes were open.

"Are you okay?"

"The cuffs. They went off after the thunder."

Rey felt his pocket for his phone, but he'd left it inside.

"I don't have the app to unlock you. I don't want to just leave you to get my phone. Can you get up?"

"I tried. I can't move."

Rey tried to get David on his feet, but he was too heavy and slippery to lift. After his second failed attempt, Rey lowered David's head back down to the turf and pea sized hail began to pelt both men. Rey covered his head with both hands and leaned over David to offer some protection. It didn't help much. Rain streamed off Rey's nose as he scanned the yard for some type of shelter. He calculated that the tool shed was about thirty feet away.

"I'm going to drag you into the shed."

"Okay."

Rey knelt behind David and wedged his hands under David's armpits and locked his fingers across his chest. Rey stood and raised David up to his waist, a move Rey learned as a corrections officer as an effective way to drag a large victim from a scene.

Rey backed up toward the shed and dragged David across the wet grass. He increased his pace with the sting of each piece of hail. A half minute later, he was at the entrance to his shed. Rey dropped one arm and opened the door while he held onto David with the other hand. Rey was happy he didn't lock the shed like Christina asked when they moved in.

Aided by the gusty wind, the door swung open and slammed against the outside of the shed. Rey pulled David out of the rain. Once inside, Rey fell backward onto the dirt floor and David landed on top of him. Rey slid out from underneath David and leaned him up against the wall of the shed. Rey moved against the wall next to David. They listened to the wind howl and the mixture of rain and hail unleash their fury on the shed roof. Neither said a word until the deafening sounds of the storm began to subside.

"I'm so sorry about this, David. I need to let John at Sectronix know. We need a way to unlock Sure Cuffs in an emergency like this."

On Monday, Rey caught John in the hallway.

"Hey, John, do you have a minute?"

John checked his watch. "Yeah, I have about ten minutes until my next meeting. What's up?"

Rey moved to the side of the hallway to allow his colleagues to pass. "We need to tweak the sound activation function on Sure Cuffs. A clap of thunder activated it over the weekend, and I had to pull David through the mud while being pelted with hail to get him out of a nasty storm. Can you alter the sound activation so that never happens to someone else?"

John leaned up against the wall. He placed his elbow in one hand and stroked his chin. After gazing at the ceiling tiles for several seconds, he responded. "Maybe we can tweak the decibel level a bit, but I'm afraid it won't pick up somebody yelling who really needs to activate Sure Cuffs."

Rey nodded. "Yeah, that's an important feature. Is there any other way?"

John turned his attention to the ceiling again and shook his head. "I can't think of anything right now."

"Give it some thought. Like all the previous changes, I'm sure this is something that will affect other RIHARP hosts, so we need to fix it now."

Rey went one direction and John went the other. Just before Rey turned down another corridor, he heard his name.

"Rey, Rey! I've got it!"

John darted back down the hall toward Rey. He was out of breath when he arrived. "I've got it."

Rey waited for John to catch his breath.

"You know how we have a secret keyword to activate Sure Cuffs?"

Rey nodded. "Yeah, that's part of the voice and sound upgrade we added."

"We can add another secret word to deactivate Sure Cuffs. Maybe we can even make it temporary, like two or three minutes and then it activates again. That'd be enough to get an inmate out of any danger but prevent them from abusing or coercing a keyword out of a RIHARP host."

Rey furrowed his brow as he contemplated John's idea. Moments later, a wide smile spread across his face. "You never cease to amaze me. It's brilliant. Let's do it."

CHAPTER FORTY

Annie, the administrative assistant for Deputy Director Scalise, arrived unannounced next to Rey's desk. He knew why she was there before she even spoke.

"Rey, Mr. Scalise would like to see you in his office."

"Now?"

"Yes, right now."

Rey stood up and twisted his torso until he heard faint cracking sounds emitting from his back. He understood he was heading into a battle. It started as soon as Rey passed through his door.

"I thought you said you understood. I thought you were going to do everything in your power to finish RIHARP early and under budget," Mr. Scalise fired off.

He waved a printed invoice to Rey as he sat down. "What's this invoice from Sectronix for? We'd never discussed—"

He stopped shaking the paper long enough to read it. "The addition of voice and audio to Sure Cuffs. What is this?"

Heat crept into Rey's neck and shoulder as he shifted his weight in the chair. "It was necessary, sir."

"Audio and voice control for virtual hand cuffs?"

"Yes, sir."

Deputy Director Scalise stared in silence at the invoice.

Rey decided it was best to share all the bad news with him. "There will be one more invoice coming for another audio password function to complete the project."

"You're kidding, right?" Mr. Scalise asked.

"No, sir. It should be the last, though."

"The last invoice was supposed to be two invoices ago." He stood up and walked to his window. "I can see it now. This isn't going to work and I'm going to get hammered for this," he whispered loud enough for anyone in his office to hear.

Ouch.

Rey stood and moved next to the deputy director. "I understand my previous commitment to deliver RIHARP early and under budget. I am still pushing hard to ensure it's ready in five months and that's why I had to make a few more investments to ensure RIHARP is not only viable, but a remarkable program for TDCJ. These last improvements were necessary for RIHARP to work for citizen hosts in the state of Texas. Every penny we've spent so far would've been wasted without them."

The redness in Mr. Scalise's face began to fade. "What about the money, Rey? I don't have five thousand dollars laying around in my budget for surprises like this."

Rey took a deep breath and then exhaled.

"I know of a way that we could find additional funds for RIHARP, but it's a little unconventional."

"How unconventional?"

"In another department."

Deputy Director Scalise raised his eyebrows and Rey shared his potential solution. Two minutes later he said he'd consider Rey's suggestion and dismissed him from his office.

His suggestion was bold, but true. Rey had to save RIHARP at all costs.

Rey spent long hours in the office analyzing the RIHARP incident reports and fine-tuning the operating procedures. He thought about spending time with Christina and the kids around the upcoming holidays. He hoped that Thanksgiving and Christmas could bring them closer as a family. Rey also let himself dream a little about a day when RIHARP was approved. Visions of Norway and Lars appeared in his mind, but they were quickly replaced by his father's face two decades ago. Vindicating his father's failure drove Rey like a magnet to metal. A lot was riding on RIHARP for Rey.

After several days, Rey still didn't hear from his boss, so he assumed he got the budget money he needed. He was in the clear now. Or so he thought.

"Mendoza!"

The voice penetrated Rey deep in his gut. It was unmistakably Lamar and he was shouting at Rey as he walked by his office.

After a deep breath, Rey skittered into his office. Lamar stood up and walked around until he could lean on the front of his desk. He crossed his arms as Rey stopped behind the chair acting as a barrier between the two men.

"Hey, Mr. Taylor, I haven't seen you—"

"Stop with the patronizing political act, Mendoza," Lamar interrupted. "You know why I called you in here."

Rey said nothing.

"How could you offer up my budget to fund your little pet project? That's low, man."

Despite a one-inch height advantage, Rey felt small next to Lamar. He could intimidate Rey like very few people could, but Rey was getting used to defending RIHARP. Courage began to well inside him as he considered the stakes of the program.

"I knew you weren't using the money. I put it in the budget to hire an outside PR firm and you approved it, but never used it. Why should that money be tied up when other departments need it?"

"What gives you the right to meddle in another department's budget? Nobody does that. People don't pick the pocket of another department's budget for some silly pet project," Lamar hissed.

Is that what Lamar thinks RIHARP is? A pet project?

"I'm sorry you don't understand the complexities of RIHARP, but it's hardly a pet project for my gratification. It will provide real reform for inmates. It may give these men and women in TDCJ facilities a much needed second chance to lead a life as productive citizens," Rey fired back.

Lamar shook his head quickly as if Rey slapped him. He took two steps toward Rey and pointed his finger at him.

"Don't lecture me on prison reform and second chances. I come from a long line of corrections professionals and I've forgotten more about this industry than you'll ever know. Here's a newsflash for you. We lock up bad guys after they commit crimes. Our job is to make sure they serve their time. That's it. We don't need to send out inmate satisfaction surveys or help make sure they enjoy their time behind bars like some two-bit motel. It's really simple. You don't need a second chance if you get it right the first time. Stop coddling these inmates and stop messing with me or you'll soon experience the painful consequences."

"This isn't personal, Mr. Taylor. It's business. The TDCJ owns the budgets, and the directors have ultimate say about how money is invested. Over time, this program could save the system millions."

Lamar glared at Rey and went behind his desk. "That is all. You can go now."

Rey shuffled out of Lamar's office. Dismissing him like he was still his boss rankled a little, but that wasn't Rey's main concern. He wasn't sure how much more Lamar could do to derail RIHARP or him personally, but Rey knew he was willing to do about anything. Rey needed to keep an eye out for Lamar's next move.

CHAPTER FORTY-ONE

The nighttime temps cooled as the sun rose later and retired earlier each day. Rey managed to avoid additional confrontations with Lamar and Deputy Director Scalise while he put in long hours at work perfecting RIHARP. He also spent considerable time with David once he got home at night. Frustration with his personal life grew as the prospect for RIHARP success slowly improved. Now that Christina was teaching full-time again, Rey was seeing her and the kids less often. Rey hoped he could change the dynamics of the Mendoza household during the holidays.

Christina's parents offered to host Thanksgiving dinner in their home north of San Antonio. Rey knew they meant well and did the best they could, but their new cozy two-bedroom home wasn't set up to entertain a party of six. Noah insisted at sitting at the small kitchen table already crowded with four adults and a full thanksgiving feast. Once room was made for Noah at the table, Maddie wanted to shoehorn a spot for herself at the miniscule table as well.

After both kids started to wine and cry, Rey moved to the family room couch and ate his turkey, stuffing, and mashed sweet potatoes by himself. He pretended to be interested in the football game on TV, but he could care less about the two teams playing after the Dallas Cowboys finished their game hours earlier.

It was even worse on Christmas. In their old San Antonio house, the Christmas tree from the thrift store consumed the corner of the family room and the area around it. It blocked several inches of the flat screen TV in the built-in niche next to the tree. This caused Rey to complain when he watched TV causing tension between him and Christina to ratchet higher every day Rey came down to visit.

On Christmas morning, Christina got upset because there wasn't enough room to take quality pictures of the kids opening the presents. Someone was always obstructing her view and she kept tripping over toys hidden under a layer of wrapping paper while she maneuvered for a better angle. Rey left after brunch to go back to Austin to check on David. It was only partially true. He also left so he didn't let his frustration boil over and cause him to say something he'd regret on Christmas Day. Long calls to his parents and brother during the drive to Austin lifted his spirits a little, but having to hide the fact he was living separately from his wife and kids left him feeling even more lonely.

The Mendoza family hit rock bottom on New Year's Eve. Despite an offer from the grandparents to watch the kids, Christina and Ray both stayed home alone. Rey watched the New Year's celebration in New York's Times Square. Tears ran down his cheeks when he saw the couples kissing on TV at midnight, a scene Rey and Christina created themselves every year for the last decade. Until this year, that is.

Rey knew something had to change. He closed his eyes, leaned back into the couch cushions and prayed. He prayed harder and longer than he could remember. After he finished, Rey was mentally exhausted. He looked at the clock on the DVR and saw it was only eleven twenty-two. He had nearly forty minutes until he could celebrate the new year.

No celebration would occur in the quiet Mendoza house. Rey fell asleep on the couch until the sun beamed through the open blinds and Rey sat up. He swung his legs over the side of the couch and buried his face in his hands.

"Happy New Year, Rey. I hope this year is better than the last."

CHAPTER FORTY-TWO

The new year didn't bring any changes the first week, but Rey received good news from Christina the second week. The teacher was returning from maternity leave and Christina only had three more weeks of full-time work to help the teacher transition back to her class. Then she would be a substitute teacher for the rest of the semester.

For the first time in months, Rey had hope.

After hearing the news, Rey was determined get his family back as soon as possible. He lay in bed on a rainy Saturday morning while he considered several options from the warmth of his bed. "That's it!" he cried, tossing off the covers and popping up. He tiptoed around dressing and getting breakfast, then left without saying a word to David.

"Do you like him?" The young woman asked through her inquisitive smile.

Rey tilted his head and pondered the question. "His breath stinks and he drew blood earlier. I'm not sure if I like him."

The smile on the shelter volunteer's face vanished. "Really?"

Rey couldn't contain his ruse. "No, I'm just kidding. I love him."

The volunteer clutched her chest. "Good. You scared me for a second there."

Rey lifted the puppy up to his face and received a few more kisses.

"What breed do you think he is?"

"We're not entirely sure. His mother was found as stray over near Lake Travis so he's definitely part poodle, and probably some terrier or a terrier-poodle mix. We don't see too many like that in here and he won't last too long."

"How much do you think he'll shed? I have a son with asthma."

The worker's eyebrows pinched closer as she examined the coat on his back and neck. "He's mostly a poodle. Probably a parti poodle with those black and white markings, so you should be fine with shedding."

Rey stared at the puppy as he pounced on a chew toy. "I'll take him."

As Rey drove home, the young puppy yelped in the crate in the crew cab behind him. It was so loud that Rey pulled over and moved the crate into the front seat to stop the ear-splitting noise. Once Rey was in his driveway, he opened the crate and carried the puppy to the backyard. He sat frozen in the same spot and sniffed the grass and air around him. Enough courage filled the young canine that he was willing to pounce a few inches to his left. He chewed at some grass and then galloped over next to Rey's shoes.

"Go on, take a look around. This is your new yard."

The puppy looked up at him as if he was speaking a language from Mars. Rey moved ten paces away. The puppy searched the area for another second before darting back to his new owner. Rey picked up a stick and tossed it. The puppy's ears sprang up, but he didn't give chase.

"Fetch. Come on, boy, go get it."

The black and white creature sat and stared up at his confusing owner.

Convinced he wasn't going to train the overwhelmed animal in one day, Rey picked up the puppy and took him inside.

Once inside, the puppy sniffed inside the perimeter of the family room. Rey sat down on the couch and observed the investigation.

Several minutes later, David emerged from his bedroom. He stopped and jumped back several steps as if he was avoiding a coiled rattlesnake. "What's that?"

Rey laughed. "That's our new puppy."

David squinted and leaned closer to the puppy that was tugging on the end of the rug. He appeared to conclude that the twenty-two-pound creature was not an immediate threat and moved next to the puppy. "Can I pet him?"

"Sure."

David knelt and patted the top of his head. The puppy turned his attention from the rug and attacked David's hand.

"Ouch!" David screeched as he yanked his hand away. He glared at the confused puppy as if he was plotting his counterattack.

"What'd he do?"

"He bit me."

"He's just playing."

"That's not playing. He bit me really hard."

Rey couldn't tell if David was joking or if he was seriously offended at the perceived attack. David's face did not display any signs of amusement.

"Have you ever owned a pet before?"

"In my house growing up? No way. My brother tried to keep a stray dog once when I was ten or eleven, but he was only around a few days."

Rey moved from the couch to the chair to get a better view of the puppy attempting to climb the coffee table.

"What happened?"

"I don't know for sure. He growled at my dad when he went into my brother's room one morning. When we got home from school later that day, he was gone. Nobody ever mentioned a dog or any kind of pet ever again."

Empathy for David filled Rey's heart. The more he learned about David's childhood, the more he realized David was not raised to succeed in life. His fate to spend time in prison was sealed long before he ever got behind the wheel that murderous night.

"What's his name?" David asked.

Rey tilted his head and looked down at the furball on the floor.

"I haven't named him yet. Got any good suggestions?"

David took a step back and raised his hands in surrender. "I don't have any good names for a dog. I don't know anything about naming an animal."

"How about we ask the kids to help name him?"

David nodded in approval and resumed his journey into the kitchen. Rey moved back to the couch and pulled his phone from his pocket. He selected Christina's number and let his thumb hover over the send button. His heart ached for one of the deep conversations he used to have with his wife. He missed her smile, her strength, and her love. Rey longed to hold his kids and hear them playing and laughing. He'd be delighted to break up a fight between his kids at this time. He pushed the button. After a few seconds of small talk, Rey told Christina he had a surprise for the kids. They agreed to meet later that evening.

Seconds after arriving, both kids dropped to the floor and began playing with the four-month old pooch when they saw him in the family room. Christina flashed Rey a look that he couldn't read. Was it happiness or disappointment? She crossed her arms and fixed her eyes on the joy plastered on the faces of her children. Christina cracked a smile when the exuberant puppy leapt up and planted several kisses on Maddie's cheek. She screamed "eww" and fell over in laughter.

"I didn't think you wanted a pet because of Noah's asthma," Christina noted while keeping her eyes on the kids.

"I've always wanted a pet, but just needed to find the right one. This one doesn't shed."

"I hope you take the time to train him if you are going to keep him in the house."

"What do you mean? Dogs have to be trained?"

Christina's head snapped up and noticed the spry smile on her husband's face.

"For a second, I thought you were serious."

"I know I've got to train him. I'm going to start him on doggy basic training tomorrow, so he'll be fully trained when you move back in."

Rey looked at Christina out of the corner of his eye. He was searching for some type of reaction to his comment on moving back in. Christina was either a good poker player or did not have a reaction to Rey's comment that he could detect.

The Mendozas hung out in the family room like they used to. The kids were distracted by the dog and Christina relaxed with a magazine on the couch.

"I'm almost done with all the construction. I'm just down to paint and some touch up."

"That's great." Christina replied without looking up.

"I had David help. It really sped everything up. You know, I think he is—"

"Daddy, what's his name?" Noah interrupted.

Rey walked over to the kids and bent down to ruffle the downy fur of their new pet. "He doesn't have a name yet. I was hoping you two could name him."

Both kids looked down as if the black and white puppy was going to shout out a name.

"Let's name him Patches," his daughter said. "It looks like he has black patches over his eyes."

"That's perfect, Maddie. What do you think, Noah?"

"He looks like a Patches."

Rey stood up. "How about you, mom? Are you good with Patches?"

Christina looked up from her magazine. "Oh, yeah. Patches is perfect."

Rey returned to his seat next to Christina on the couch.

"Now where were we? I think we were discussing when you and the kids would be moving back." Rey proclaimed with a hopeful grin.

Christina crossed her arms and legs. "I still have a couple more weeks at Castle Hill."

Rey's grin quickly faded.

"Plus, you still aren't done with all the construction. Let's talk about this after I'm done at Castle Hill and you are one hundred percent done with the construction."

He nodded but wondered why she was so reticent to commit to a date.

Christina called to the kids, "Say good-bye to Patches. We have to drive back and need to leave now."

"Aww. Can we stay and play with Patches a while longer?" Maddie asked.

"Not tonight."

Both kids left full of giggles and smiles.

It was just the sound Rey needed to hear.

CHAPTER FORTY-THREE

After an eventful day, Rey went to bed early. Instead of falling asleep, he lay in bed thinking about his next steps. He tossed and turned for ninety minutes and finally fell asleep sometime after midnight.

A strange noise woke Rey and he shot up in bed. Was that a baby crying?

He turned his head and slowed his breathing. The house was quiet, so Rey lay back down. His alarm clock read one thirty-three.

Next Rey heard a whimper. He recognized the sound this time. It was Patches calling Rey for one of his multiple midnight potty breaks.

Rey chuckled. The whine and cry of Patches took Rey back to when Noah and Maddie needed every-two-hour feedings after they came home from the hospital. He tried to forget the exhaustion he endured as he took every other feeding shift to let Christina sleep. Now, he had to get up every few hours with Patches to let him go outside.

Later that week, Patches had his first accident inside the house and Rey didn't want to have to clean up another mess. However, once Patches got outside, he didn't want to go to the bathroom, he wanted to play. This routine went on for days and Rey was not making any progress. He was getting more exhausted and frustrated with his stubborn pet.

Then Patches began using the family room rug as his bathroom. He wasn't used to holding it that long while Rey was at work. Rey found an online article that recommended crate training, so he pulled Patches's travel crate out of the shed and set it up in the kitchen.

Rey started the crate training before he went to work. He left work a few minutes early so Patches wouldn't be in the crate too long the first day. During his walk across the parking lot, visions of another mess waiting for him at home filled his mind. Rey closed the truck door and looked in the rear-view mirror. The blood-shot eyes and haggard look was the image of a defeated man.

Rey inserted his key but did not turn the ignition. Instead, he scrolled through his phone until he found Captain Maxwell in his contacts. He started the truck and hit send.

Captain Maxwell answered as Rey pulled out of the parking lot. After a minute of catching up, Rey shared his frustration with his new puppy. "You and Pastor Scott said it would be a good idea, but it's not working. Patches is a great pet, but he doesn't do what I tell him. He still pees in the house almost every day."

Captain Maxell chuckled. "It's a lot of work to train a puppy. Especially with just the two of you living in the house. That makes it even harder on the both of you."

"Both of us? I'm the only one training Patches."

"Do you still have the guy from prison living with you?"

"Yeah, David is still living with me, but I'm the only one training Patches."

Captain Maxwell laughed. "Well, there's your problem, Rey."

"How's that my problem?"

"Don't you think making him responsible for someone other

than himself would be a good idea? That's what Pastor Scott and I were telling you in the coffee shop. The dog was for David, not you. I think you got Patches for the wrong reasons."

Rey was silent.

Captain Maxwell cleared his throat. "I think it would be helpful for David to gain a sense of responsibility and accountability by putting him in charge of the dog. Let David train him. It may help both David and your puppy adhere to your house rules and learn responsibility. Does that make sense?"

"Yeah, it makes sense when you put it that way."

"Rey, this David fellow needs some self-confidence. He must trust himself first and then trust others to ever share love. Yes, trusting others can open their lives to pain, but it's the only way to experience true love. I sense that's something he's never felt in his life."

Rey thanked his long-time friend and mentor. He considered everything Captain Maxwell said the rest of the way home. When Rey arrived home and walked into the house, he saw Patches jumping wildly in his crate and took him outside for a walk. Rey found another accident in the crate.

The next morning, Rey changed clothes and took Patches out before he had another accident. Patches sniffed, pulled and frolicked during the walk, but never went to the bathroom. Five minutes after they returned to the house, Rey caught Patches peeing on the family room rug like he'd done multiple times in the past.

"No! No Patches!" Rey roared.

The black and white dog pulled his short tail between his legs and ran into the kitchen. Rey's shoulders slumped and he followed Patches. He leaned down to comfort the shivering dog.

"I'm sorry, I didn't mean to yell at you. You can't go to the bathroom inside. You need to go outside."

Rey left after Patches appeared to relax. He walked into his bathroom and splashed cool water on his face. He thought more about the conversation with Captain Maxwell.

Why is it so hard for me to trust David with training Patches? How am I ever going to help David believe in himself if I don't believe in him?

Rey left his room and found David in the kitchen and Patches on the couch.

"Patches, get down."

Patches lowered his head but did not budge.

"He seems to like the couch." David said as he entered the family room.

"I'm sure he does, but I don't want him on the furniture. Noah will be back here soon and Patches has his own dog bed."

"The couch is a lot more comfortable, though."

Rey faced David. "It would be nice if you could help reinforce his training instead of constantly watching him break the rules. He thinks it's okay when you don't support what I tell him."

"You want me to help?"

"Yes, I want you to help."

"Do you want me to help train him?"

Rey tilted his head, "Why do you think you could help train him when I can't?"

David smiled. "Time. I'm here with him all day so I can take the time to make sure he goes to the bathroom outside, exercise him and keep him off the furniture. You are in too much of a rush before work and before you go to bed. I have nothing but time."

Rey's eyebrows drew in. He knew David made a valid argument and he really needed his help. "Okay, yes! I want you to help train him." It felt good to finally say it.

David's eyes widened at the response. "Okay, but I'm not sure how."

"I'm going to help with the steps to train him, but you'll be in charge of training Patches. I'll print out some of the tips and techniques I found online that you can use."

Rey observed the widest smile he'd ever seen from David. He already knew he made the right decision.

CHAPTER FORTY-FOUR

Soon after David took on the responsibility to train Patches, it was rare to see David apart from his new canine pupil. The positive response was almost immediate. David got up earlier to spend time with Patches in the backyard and stayed out later with him to ensure he went to the bathroom. One morning, Rey caught David standing in the rain with Patches before he left for work.

A month later, the significant growth of Patches was obvious. He hadn't had an accident in weeks and stopped jumping on the furniture. Rey also noticed positive changes in his RIHARP guest. David was following the house rules and even doing more than was asked.

It never occurred to Rey that Patches kept going to the bathroom on the rug because of the scent. One afternoon, Rey came home from work and found the area rug from the family room missing. It was draped over the swing set in the backyard. David had scrubbed it and hosed it down until the scent of Patches's accidents was gone.

The dramatic changes by Rey's housemate inspired him. On Wednesdays, he started going directly to his old San Antonio house after work. He would prepare a meal for everyone and then take Noah and Maddie to a sprawling city park.

One evening after Rey worked well past eight o'clock, he arrived home and opened the refrigerator to search for a quick meal. Inside he found a plate of scrambled eggs, bacon and toast ready to be reheated.

Rey also noticed that Patches no longer greeted him at the door, so he sent out to find what was distracting his furry friend. Patches wasn't in the kitchen or the family room. Rey noticed the light was on in David's room, so he tiptoed over to get a better look. What he saw stopped Rey in his tracks.

David was sitting on the floor next to an outstretched towel. Patches was lying on the towel next to David while he gently brushed the pup's curly fur. David whispered to Patches with each stroke of the brush. Rey couldn't hear what David was saying, but the affection of their tight bond radiated from them.

Later that evening, Rey closed his laptop and strolled back to David's room. "Hey David, I'm going to sit outside on the porch to enjoy this great February weather. Care to join me?"

David's face lit up. He pointed the remote control to the TV and powered it off. "Sure. Let me get dressed and grab a jacket. I'll be out in a minute."

Rey took his usual seat to the right of the bistro table. It provided the best view of the street in front of their house. Two minutes later, David joined him. He sat in the chair usually reserved for Christina.

Rey and David looked over the quiet street. Neither spoke, until Rey broke the silence. "You and Patches seem to be getting along great."

"Yeah," David said with a wide smile.

"He's doing great now. He's changed so much for the better since you've been training him."

"That stubborn little guy was no match for me. He doesn't know stubborn like I do."

Rey laughed and took a drink of his sparkling water. "I've also noticed a big change in you."

David continued to scan the street and did not reply.

"It's been a positive change."

David looked down at the painted pine planks on the front porch. "Thanks."

Rey leaned closer to David. "Why do you think Patches had that impact on you?"

David looked out toward the street again. This time he was looking over the houses and trees as if he were searching for the right answer. "I've never felt loyalty like that. He doesn't care about my past or what I look like. He loves me just the way I am."

Rey leaned closer. "Sounds a lot like Jesus."

David shook his head, "I don't know. I've heard some of the other guys at Huntsville talk about Jesus, but I didn't hear much about love. 'Repent, repent!' they'd say. I heard about a lot of rules and judgment. Especially for guys like me."

Rey smiled. "Do you know Jesus died for your sins because he loves you just the way you are? He died on the cross so you can have peace with God and eternal life in Heaven. You just have to accept Jesus as your Savior, ask for forgiveness for your sins and allow Him into your heart. Have you heard that story?"

David leaned back and stared out into the yard for a few seconds. "Give me eternal life in Heaven? A guy in jail for murder? I'm not buying it."

"Have you ever heard of Moses or David in the Bible?"

"Yeah."

"Moses murdered an Egyptian and David had one of his soldiers killed so he could take his wife. I feel pretty confident they are in Heaven."

David's eyebrows nearly joined above his nose and he shook his head. "I didn't know that. I didn't think a guy like me could ever get to Heaven."

"Jesus died on the cross to save all of us, even when we didn't deserve it. He died for *all* of us, not just some people that are better at following the rules. It's called grace and it's been extended to everyone. We just have to choose to receive it."

Rey maintained his gaze on David, but he did not respond.

Rey could picture the gears turning inside of David's head trying to process this mind-blowing revelation.

"Do you want to hear more?"

"If it's not all about rules and judgment, I'm all ears."

The two men talked for another hour on the front porch. Rey caught David quickly swiping away a tear more than once.

Rey patted David on this shoulder. "I'm heading in now. Come in whenever you are ready."

David looked up. He wiped his bloodshot eyes. "I have something I need to tell you."

Rey looked at his phone. It was two hours past his normal bedtime. "It's getting late. Can you tell me tomorrow?"

"It's about why I was charged with assaulting a minor."

Rey pulled a chair next to David. "Okay, I have as much time as you need."

Rey returned to work the next day in a fog. His conversation with David resulted in so many conflicting emotions. However, Rey was forced to snap back to his current reality as soon as his calendar popped up on his screen.

Deputy Director Scalise filled his calendar with meetings in preparation for the final review of RIHARP. It was the one and only time to present RIHARP to TDCJ senior directors so they could vote to kill it or extend it to citizens of Texas.

For the next two weeks, Rey and the Project Second Chance team worked late every day to ensure all their facts, figures, and insights reflected the promising progress of RIHARP. They had to convince the senior officials that RIHARP is ready for the real world. The last year of their lives and their jobs depended on it.

Rey wasn't spending much time with David. He missed the dinners with David and watching the two best friends play in the yard before work. Once Rey was able to take a break on the weekend, he noticed a change in David.

David became withdrawn and appeared to be avoiding Rey. He spent much of his time with Patches in his room.

Did I push David too far with the new Bible I placed on his dresser earlier this week? Did his story of assaulting a minor bring up old wounds he wasn't ready to face?

Rey committed to giving David his space to figure things out. He planned to invite him outside again to talk once his schedule got back to normal. He wanted David to feel comfortable enough to ask questions or share concerns about their previous conversation. He prayed God would continue working in David's heart.

Four days before the big presentation, Rey worked with the team late into the evening. He left the TDCJ office after nine and was exhausted from the cumulation of long days and the Chinese food that didn't seem to agree with him. He rubbed his eyes and began the journey on the quiet streets back to his house.

After Rey turned down his street, a parked vehicle caught his attention. It was white panel van parked in front of the home of an elderly couple he'd met when they moved in. The van had a dented front corner panel and was losing its battle against rust. A man was sitting in the driver's seat with the engine running. A flood of observations and questions ran through Rey's head in the span of one house.

It's too late for any kind of service call.

There wasn't a company logo on the van.

Is that man by himself?

Was he planning to break into their house?

As Rey continued to think and roll down the street, movement caught his eye. He stretched his neck and caught the silhouette of a person before he disappeared behind the shadows in a side yard. The hair on Rey's neck stood up.

He was in Rey's yard.

CHAPTER FORTY-FIVE

Rey engaged his brakes and pulled to the curb in one motion. He was fully alert now and his heart pounded inside his chest. He opened his glovebox to retrieve his pistol but was reminded by its absence that he locked it in his gun safe months ago, when David first moved in. He was going to have to approach this person unarmed.

He killed the engine and crept out of his car. Gently Rey pushed the car door shut, slowing to an inch per second until he heard a faint click. He waited until the dome light turned off before making his next move.

Rey bounded toward his house in the shadows cast by the decades-old live oak trees. Settling between two overgrown shrubs, he caught a glimpse of the van driver in his side mirror. He was looking at his phone.

Rey felt his pulse beating stronger in his neck with every step. This was like a SORT extraction back in his days at Torres prison, but without the protective gear and backup. Rey didn't know if the man was armed with a knife or gun. Regardless, he was committed to resolving the situation. He needed to catch the person trying to break into his home.

The figure never returned from the shadows on the side of the house.

Is he inside? Is David in danger?

Rey entered his yard from the opposite side of the house, taking each step with care in order to not make a sound. Once he reached the area where the person vanished, Rey peeked around the corner. His heart sank. A man was talking to David through the window.

Rey took a deep breath to slow his breathing so he could hear the conversation.

"I told you I was coming, so where is it?" The question came from a voice Rey did not recognize.

"I said not to come tonight. He could be home anytime," David whispered back.

"I told you we need some cash."

"I don't have any to give you."

"You better find something fast 'cause I aint leaving empty handed."

Rey blinked and shook his head.

Was this guy coming to David for cash? David doesn't have any money so why is he coming to him?

The answer hit Rey like a speeding freight train. The adrenaline burst in his stomach hit first and the nauseous sensation followed. Rey trusted David, at least as much as he could trust a convicted felon. He was even starting to like him. Disappointment washed over Rey.

Anger quickly followed. Rey turned his attention to the trespasser in his yard. Every muscle in Rey's body tensed. He crouched down and counted down from five in his head.

Five, four, three, two, one.

Rey pounced and was steps from the man before he even noticed him. He turned to run, but it was too late. Rey was on top of him like a leopard dropping from a branch onto a gazelle. He tackled the man in the grass before he could take his third step. All of Rey's weight concentrated into the man's back, causing a loud thud to echo between the homes. He quickly pulled the man's arms behind his back. The man did not resist as he gasped for air.

Rey turned the man on his side but kept his arms behind his back. This allowed the man to get enough air to prevent him from hyperventilating. A half minute later, the man's breathing slowed from the rapid panting of seconds earlier.

"Get up!" Rey commanded as he helped the man get to his feet.

David watched through the open window the whole time. His jaw was open as he leaned slightly out of the window to see the man on the ground.

"David, what's going on here?"

"Nothing."

"Don't lie to me," Rey roared. "I heard you two talking about money. What are you giving him? Did you steal money or something else?

"I didn't steal anything," David whispered.

"Then why is this man here?"

David's forehead wrinkled. "He's been emailing me and asking to get him cash or something he can sell fast for a couple weeks now."

"How do you know this guy?"

"We met in Huntsville years ago and he was released last month. He's from Bee Cave and he knew I was living in Austin, so he tracked me down. I kept telling him that I wasn't going to help him, but he found me and knocked on my window a few minutes ago."

Rey recalled hearing David telling the man not to come. Rey turned his attention to the man he secured. His pulse and breathing were now closer to normal. "Is that true?"

"Nah, man this guy owes me money. I ain't looking to steal nothing. Just collecting what is rightfully mine."

"Right. Just like your buddy in the van is waiting to take his grandma to church."

The man's eyes widened at Rey's sarcasm.

"Yeah, that's right. I got his plate number when I was pulling in."

The man turned to David. "You better not rat on me."

Rey slammed the man up against the house. "He's not the one you need to worry about."

The man tried to maneuver out of Rey's grip. Rey pushed his hands further up his back until he stopped.

Rey turned the man toward the van. He pushed him and they both began to walk. When they got within thirty feet of the van, Rey noticed the driver was still looking at his phone.

Rey chuckled to himself. "Some getaway driver."

His captive grunted.

"I'll know both of your identities by morning. If I ever hear of either of you contacting David or coming within five miles of my house, I'll have every deputy in Travis County hunting you down. I'm sure you're violating several stipulations of your parole. So unless you want to spend more time behind bars, you better get out of here as fast as you can."

Rey gave the man a firm shove toward the van and let go of him. He took several steps toward the van and turned around. Rey positioned himself for a counterattack, but it never came. The man opened the passenger door to the van and Rey saw in the side mirror that the driver finally looked up from his phone. He looked to the man in the passenger seat and then in the mirror at the silhouette behind the van. A second later, the van squealed its tires as it zipped away and turned onto the next cross street.

David was waiting in the kitchen when Rey returned.

"I'm sorry, Rey. I kept telling him I wasn't going to help him, but he just kept on asking."

"David, you should have told me. I could have helped."

David's chin dropped to his chest. His eyes fixed on the floor. "I didn't think it would come to this. I kept telling him no."

"Okay, if anything like this happens in the future, you need to tell me or someone else right away. A misunderstanding can land you back in Huntsville. These are the kinds of things you need to do when you are free someday. Do you understand?"

David nodded. "Yes. Yes, I do."

"I'm curious. Why didn't you want to help this guy?"

David looked up from the floor. His face was ashen. "Because Jesus forgave me for what I did, and I don't want to do anything else to disappoint him."

Those words traveled to the center of Rey's heart. He was filled with the most hope he had for David since he arrived.

CHAPTER FORTY-SIX

The next morning, Rey arrived in the office thirty minutes late. He could tell something was wrong with the way everyone on his floor was acting.

Was I in trouble for coming in a little late after working into the night?

He searched for his team and found Carrie talking to several people near the coffee station. She noticed Rey and left the group.

"You just getting in?"

"Yeah, what's going on? Nobody is at their desk."

"You didn't hear yet?"

"Hear what?"

Carrie's eyes widened and a smile exposed her pale dimples. "Lamar Taylor got into a confrontation with his inmate last night. He notified his counselor, saying Lamar is verbally abusive and it finally got physical."

Rey's jaw dropped. He was shocked but not surprised. He guessed Lamar could push anyone to snap.

"Wow, I wasn't expecting to hear that when I walked in today. Where's everyone now?"

"Mr. Scalise called an emergency meeting after he ordered the inmate shipped back to prison and banned Lamar from participating in RIHARP. I heard they are starting an investigation into the abuse and Lamar's potential termination. He'd made threats against several members of his own team in communications."

Rey felt sorry for the inmate. He didn't get a fair shot at succeeding outside of prison with Lamar as his RIHARP host. But he felt worse that he hadn't reported Lamar's threats to HR months ago. He assumed Lamar was targeting him alone.

When Rey walked down the hall, he noticed Lamar standing behind his desk in his office. Rey passed by and then stopped. He turned into Lamar's office marched right up to his desk.

Lamar stopped placing items into the banker's box on his desk and held up his hand for Rey to stop.

"Not now Rey. I've got to pack up and I don't want to hear your gloating about how karma got me. You can do a little dance if they fire me." Lamar said as he grabbed another book from the shelf.

"I have every right to be glad that you are getting a taste of your own medicine and to feel vindicated if you are fired, but I don't."

Lamar put the book in the box and looked up at Rey.

"My plan from the beginning was to give a second chance to inmates so they don't all end up back in our prisons. It wasn't ever about you – or me. I didn't realize it at first, but now I believe it was God's plan to put the most difficult inmate with me. David is thriving because of RIHARP and I'm not sorry to have had him assigned to live in my house."

Rey walked around the desk and stopped feet from Lamar. He extended his hand. Lamar did a double take at Rey's hand. He tentatively shook it.

"I hope you can overcome whatever demons are haunting you and causing your bitterness. I wish you nothing but good luck in your next endeavor. I'll be praying for you."

Rey turned to leave, and Lamar fell back in his chair. Rey never turned around, but he could picture the look of shock and confusion on his face. He just hoped this event was enough to change Lamar.

That night Rey turned his attention from Lamar back to the storms in his life. He asked Christina to bring the kids up for a family dinner.

She declined, but Rey wasn't accepting no for an answer this time. He texted her back.

I have something important to tell you. Plus, Patches really misses the kids. Can you bring them over for a little bit to spend time with Patches?

Nice guilt trip! Was her reply.

Did it work?

As long as everyone is feeling okay, we'll see you on Sunday.

Rey prepared Noah and Maddie's favorite meal. Spaghetti with light red sauce and garlic bread. After finishing their early dinner, Rey cleaned up the plates and transferred everything to the sink.

"Why don't you two go play with Patches in the family room."

They darted into the next room and the happy sounds of play erupted between the kids and their canine companion.

"They sure love that little guy," Rey observed.

"Yes, they do."

Rey moved his chair to sit closer to Christina. He reached across the table and took her hand. She leaned back slightly but did not pull her hand away.

"I invited you over tonight so we could talk. I'd like for you and the kids to move back in. I miss you."

"We miss you too, but its more than that. I need to feel safe here."

"David has grown so much since you first met him. He's a new man now. You'll notice as soon as you move back in."

Christina sighed. "Oh, Rey."

Rey put his other hand on top of hers. "He accepted Christ into his life."

Christina's head snapped up and she locked eyes with Rey. She did not say anything, but Rey could read the joy in her eyes. They both understood the power of salvation to change even the most lost souls.

"That's a step in the right direction, but I still have so many questions. So many concerns before I would bring Noah and Maddie back here."

"I understand, but can we try?"

"I want to give David a second chance, but it's not easy. His past gives me anxiety and that is not something I can just turn off. It's going to take time."

"I know, but let's do it together in the same house with everyone under the same roof."

Christina stood up and leaned against the kitchen counter. It was quiet in the kitchen. It was also quiet in the family room.

"Where are the kids?" she asked with alarm,

"I don't know, they were just in the family room a few minutes ago," Rey replied as he walked over to the empty room.

"Where's David?"

CHAPTER FORTY-SEVEN

Christina walked into the family room and saw it was empty. She trotted down the hall and checked Maddie's room and then Noah's. She rushed down to the end of the hallway and searched the master bedroom.

A hot burst of adrenaline released in her stomach and quickly traveled up her throat. *Where were they? Why didn't I keep my eye on them when they were with David?*

Christina scampered back to the beginning of the hallway and saw that David's door was wide open. He was also missing.

Tears welled up in Christina as her greatest fears crept into her thoughts. *What if he has both kids? What if he hurts them?*

She started to wonder what life would be like if anything happened to one of her kids. One of the tears escaped and landed on the hardwood floor outside of David's room.

Her chest tightened at the thought of her kids outside, alone with David. She darted to the back door but stopped before she turned the knob. A scream came from outside and Christina could identify that voice anywhere. It was Maddie. Christina turned the knob and pulled open the door in one motion. She froze when she saw David with the kids in the backyard.

David was laying on his back grasping both kids as they tried to wiggle free.

"Oh, no," she whispered. Her throat was too tight to scream.

Christina willed her legs to move. She needed to save her children. After one step, she heard a noise that shocked her. Noah and Maddie were squealing with glee.

"Let's keep him down, Noah. Don't let him get up."

"No! Stop! No more kisses!" David yelled at Patches, which generated deeper belly laughs from the young Mendozas. The three of them laughed hysterically at the relentless puppy kisses.

Rey followed Christina by a few seconds out the back door. The door slammed behind him, and everyone stopped. All eyes turned to Christina. She stared at David without blinking.

Christina felt Rey grasp her arm, but she shrugged it off and began marching toward David. Ten paces later, she towered over David and her children still lying in the grass. They had looks of confusion on their face as they peered up at the outline of their mother blocking the bright indigo sky behind her.

Christina lowered herself to one knee and rolled over on her back near David. Her shoulder pressed against his.

Confusion on Maddie and Noah's faces turned to smiles and they crawled over to their mother. Patches soon followed and planted a dozen kisses on Christina's nose, lips and cheeks in less than a minute. Giggles from Noah and Maddie filled the air again.

Christina turned her head toward David who continued to lie in the grass. She reached out and touched his arm.

"Thank you," Christina whispered.

David smiled and they both looked up at the puffy clouds dancing on the giant blue stage while they listened to the sound of happiness.

Minutes later, Christina stood up and moved to the front porch with Rey and two glasses of sweet tea while David, Patches, and the kids continued to play in the backyard.

They sat quietly on the porch for a minute. Rey grabbed

Christina's hand as they watched the neighbors going about their daily lives.

"What happened back there?" Rey asked.

Christina smiled. "It just hit me out of nowhere. One minute I was looking to save my kids from a bad guy and then I saw David lying in the grass and playing with them. Innocent and child-like. Right then I felt the changes the Holy Spirit has made in David. I let go of my fear and accepted him as he is. A new brother in Christ."

Rey slung both arms around his wife. They embraced for a half minute.

Rey pulled away and asked, "I was about to tell you about David's charge for assaulting a minor. Do you still want to know?"

Christina's smile evaporated. "I don't know. This was hard enough as it is. I don't want a setback so soon."

"I think you may actually want to hear it."

Christina tilted her head. "Okay, now I need to know the story."

CHAPTER FORTY-EIGHT

Rey cleared his throat.

"He told me that a few months before the drive-by shooting, his cousin came to him and said that another kid was bullying him. His cousin was thirteen and the bully was sixteen. David told his cousin to stand up for himself, but his cousin was afraid of the older and much bigger boy. One night after his cousin came home with a fat lip, David drove his cousin around town to find the bully. He caught up with the bully leaving a fast food restaurant and confronted him in the parking lot. David got in his face and told him to leave his cousin alone. When the bully started to laugh, David lost control. He pushed the bully and swept his legs at the same time. The bully lost all his food when he landed on his back. David jumped on him and put his forearm across his throat and told him the next time, he'd be leaving in an ambulance."

Rey took a long drink of tea before continuing. "The police were waiting for David when he dropped off his cousin at home. He was scheduled to appear for his assault trial when the murder charge hit a few months later. After David was convicted for murder, the district attorney offered him a deal for time served to plead guilty to the assault against a minor, so he did."

Christina shook her head. "Wow. I was expecting a very different story."

"I know. He committed a serious crime against that young man, but I do feel more comfortable with him and the kids."

"Why was it such a big secret?" Christina asked. "He allowed us to think the worst."

"I asked him. He said he was embarrassed. Beating up a kid, for any reason, doesn't make you a lot of friends in any social circles, including inmates. He's sorry that he did it and never told anyone else about the incident."

Rey and Christina turned back to the street. They watched a young couple walk their two dogs on the sidewalk.

"We're going to move back in," Christina blurted.

Rey did a double take. "You will?"

Christina smiled and nodded. "Yes, we will."

Rey leapt up and put his arms around Christina. Then he started pacing across the porch, muttering to himself. "I can take off work, rent a big truck."

Christina laughed. "When should we move back?"

"As soon as possible is my preference. Easter is just a few weeks away, and I'd love to hide the eggs for the kids. I've had a year to identify the best spots."

"That would be nice, but it's a lot to move and the kids will have to change schools at the end of the year. Maybe we should wait."

Rey paused. "I have a very important meeting tomorrow. Probably the most important meeting of my career so I'd love to know you are coming back soon. Knowing that would be a big help to me."

A wide smile formed on Christina's face. "Okay, let's do it."

Rey squeezed her shoulder. "Great. I'll take off a couple of days later in the week and we'll get everything moved back in. Both kids are doing great in school, so they'll catch on right away."

Christina rose and turned to head back inside.

"I have one more thing I want to discuss," he called after her.

"There's more? I'm not sure how much more I can take in one day," Christina replied with a chuckle.

"I'm sorry about all this. I hate that I may have put my desire to make a difference for others above us. I've made decisions that caused our family to be apart for the last eighteen months."

Christina let go of the door, walked back to Rey, and whispered in his ear, "I love that about you. We'll do it together from now on."

CHAPTER FORTY-NINE

An alarm was not needed to rouse Rey for his important day. He woke up forty minutes before his alarm and got ready for work. Once he was in his truck, he closed his eyes before he turned the ignition. He prayed hard for a positive result.

That morning, Rey and the Project Second Chance team crammed for their presentation like a final exam in college. After lunch, Rey went into the conference room he'd present in later that day. He strolled around the table and pictured every important person in the room. The quiet room inspired Rey. It felt like the empty stadium before a professional football championship game. It was all or nothing in that game—the same stakes Rey faced in this room.

The team huddled together near Rey's desk as the senior directors trickled in from other floors in the building and even other cities throughout Texas. The team could hear directors greet each other and take their seats in anticipation of the upcoming presentation. Five minutes before two, Rey and his team entered the room. They set up the presentation and strategically positioned themselves in the boardroom.

Deputy Director Scalise broke the silence in the room with an introduction of himself, the team and the project. Next, each member of the Project Second Chance team recapped the results from RIHARP over the previous ten months. They outlined all the improvements and the benefits to the inmates, staff, TDCJ, and the community.

Rey was last to speak. He recapped the benefits of RIHARP and looked over the room. One director's head was nodding as he struggled to stay awake while others returned blank stares.

They don't look very impressed, Rey thought.

Next, he threw them a curveball that nobody in the room was expecting. "Last, I recommend we pay the hosts to take inmates into their homes. This will allow RIHARP to recruit and retain the top hosts throughout Texas to ensure the long-term success of the program."

That woke up the room.

"How much are you talking about?" Was shouted from an unknown director.

"We'd pay them the same amount it costs us to detain, house, feed and care for inmates on a monthly basis." Rey replied.

"How can TDCJ afford to pay all these hosts? I thought you wanted this program to succeed."

Several chuckles were audible in the room. Rey realized that the question had come from the finance director.

"Sir, if we are no longer housing the inmates in our facilities, we no longer incur the expense. If we transfer, seventy, eighty or even ninety percent of the cost to the hosts, it will be a benefit to all parties. It will be a break-even program with improved rates of host recruiting and retention, which will be important for RIHARP to be successful."

Rey paused for a moment to let that sink in but continued before someone else could ask a question. "I've also calculated the benefit to the State of Texas in the form of new tax revenues if more inmates can be rehabilitated into productive citizens. Tax paying citizens!"

Rey handed a stack of paper to a board member seated near him. "Please pass these around. This shows the potential tax revenue by percentage of inmates that return to the workforce. You'll see that if even ten percent of inmates can return to the workforce, the state will see a generous return on tax revenue, and I expect RIHARP will deliver much more than ten percent."

The final slide with a big 'Thank You' appeared on the screen.

"Thank you all for your time today. Does anyone have a question?"

Rey smiled and scanned the room. He just delivered the home run speech he'd been working on for weeks. In his mind, he should start to see visible signs of excitement and a clear indication that RIHARP would be approved in the room—a standing ovation, a few high fives, or perhaps a marching band would enter soon. None of that happened.

A couple of directors quickly whispered to each other while the others maintained their stoic poker faces. After several seconds of silence, the TDCJ chief of staff spoke up.

"I don't think we have any questions, so the Project Second Chance team is free to leave now so we can discuss and vote on RIHARP."

Rey's head dropped in defeat. He could feel the lack of support in the room as he picked up his portfolio and turned to the door.

"Wait, I have one question."

Rey turned to see a silver haired woman in a navy-blue pant suit with her hand raised—the director of personnel. "We heard stories about a few incidents and improvement to the technology, but did RIHARP actually work? Does anyone have a success story they can share?"

Members of the Project Second Chance team exchanged glances. A few shook their heads or shrugged their shoulders.

"I do." Rey stepped back to the front of the boardroom.

Several of the board members that were standing sat back down.

Once everyone was settled again, Rey began. "I got the worst inmate of the group. He was the only one convicted of murder among all the inmates in this pilot program. In fact, he was convicted of three murders and child abuse."

The director of personnel's eyes widened while she put her hand over her mouth.

"My wife and kids were still living in San Antonio with plans to move to Austin with me when my inmate, David, arrived. After meeting him, my wife didn't feel comfortable living there with David in the house and at first, she was probably right. I got into multiple physical confrontations with him that led to many of the improvements to Sure Cuffs that you were briefed on earlier. It didn't happen overnight, but slowly David began to change. He started to act less like an inmate and more like a man accountable for his actions."

Rey took a drink and continued. "David wasn't the only one that changed in the last ten months. I changed too. I realized that I had to start treating him differently. I had to give him more trust, freedom, and responsibility. I had to show him love. Those are all things they need to succeed outside of prison, but never get inside our facilities. David grew so much that he trained a puppy that I couldn't, he helped me with home repairs, and he cooked dinner for me when I came home late from work. He gave his life to Jesus. He's a different man. My wife and kids feel so comfortable with David now that they are moving back in. So, would I call David an example of RIHARP success? Absolutely!"

The same poker faces were evident when Rey scanned the room until he found John from Sectronix at the far end of the table. He curled his hand into a fist and nodded.

Rey was happy with his performance. Like the football player at the end of the championship game, Rey left it all out on the field. He did everything he could to convince the board to approve RIHARP.

The chief of staff rose again. "Thank you, Mr. Mendoza. I believe the directors are ready to discuss the future of RIHARP now. We'll let you know when we've come to a decision."

The Project Second Chance team left the board room. They

gathered in a smaller conference room down the hall. One by one, they recounted the highlights and lowlights of their presentation and offered their opinion on whether or not it would get approved. The consensus was that they would come up short of approval.

An hour later, the team saw the chief of staff escorting two board members to the elevator.

"What's going on? Why are the leaving?" Rey asked.

"They have to get to the airport to catch their flights," a team member responded.

They watched the chief of staff return to the boardroom.

Two hours after the meeting ended, it was five o'clock and most of the people in the TDCJ office were leaving, but the board was still deliberating about RIHARP.

"You can all go home now if you want," Rey told the team.

They collectively responded that they were not going anywhere until they had an answer.

Suddenly, the boardroom doors opened, and everyone exited the room. They herded together toward the elevators. Several seconds after a ding, they were all gone.

The room was quiet after the elevator door closed. A growling stomach was the only sound in the room. They all knew what their quick departure meant, but one Project Second Chance team member asked anyway.

"What does this mean? Did they cancel RIHARP?"

Rey put his hand on his shoulder and shook his head. "We gave it our all. I'm so sorry."

CHAPTER FIFTY

Shocked, Rey drifted back to his desk. He thought the team delivered an amazing presentation and made a compelling case to approve RIHARP. His mind was elsewhere as he packed to go home until the chime on his phone brought him back to reality.

It was a text from Deputy Director Scalise: *Please come down to the board room now.*

Rey was already moving before he finished reading the text. While his eyes adjusted to the darker room, he was smacked by the scent of coffee wafting throughout the room. The air was thick and stagnant, as if a long mental battle had just concluded.

"Grab a chair, Rey," the deputy director said as he motioned to a leather chair next to him. The senior director of IT and the director of personnel were also in the room. Rey didn't even notice that they never left the board meeting with the others.

"The board has voted and hammered out some additional details. We wanted you to be here for this," Deputy Director Scalise explained.

Rey nodded.

Ronald Green, the senior director of IT cleared his throat. "Per unanimous vote, RIHARP passes and will be available to the citizens of Texas on the first of the month. Screening of qualified inmates and recruiting of hosts will begin immediately. The board has authorized a new position of Community Relations Director to lead the RIHARP efforts with the public."

Rey smiled wide as he straightened up in his seat.

"The board agreed that you are the ideal candidate and should be appointed to this position, Director Green declared. "It will not be posted; it is your position today if you choose to accept it."

Rey turned to Deputy Director Scalise, who smiled and nodded.

"Yes, I'll take the new position!"

The four discussed the next steps for RIHARP. When they finished, Rey shook their hands and left the board room. Mr. Scalise caught up with him as he scampered back to his desk.

"Congratulations! Your team knocked this one out of the park."

"Thank you, sir. We put in a lot of long days and nights to make this all happen."

"Your financial analysis with the tax benefit threw us all for a nice loop. Where did you come up with that idea?"

"It's amazing what a lack of sleep and sheer determination can do for the mind," Rey replied with a chuckle.

"Well, whatever it was, it helped, as did with your personal story. Keep up the good work."

Deputy Director Scalise left Rey alone at his desk. His thoughts turned to Christina and his father. He hoped they'd both be thrilled with the victory they achieved today.

When Rey arrived at his truck in the empty TDCJ parking lot, he looked at his watch. It was six thirty, so his parents were probably just getting ready for dinner. He found his father's number and hit send.

"Hi, Papa. I have some exciting new to share. Do you have a minute?"

"Sure, son, what is it?"

Rey recounted all the details of the RIHARP presentation at the board meeting. He beamed with excitement when he shared that inmates in Texas will experience the same type of rights and freedoms that his father fought for two decades earlier.

"We did it. It took twenty years, but we did it."

Rodolfo Mendoza was silent on his end of the line. Rey grew concerned.

"Hello? Papa, are you there?"

A sniffle was all Rey heard, but that's all he needed to hear.

"I also got a promotion to director. They want me to help spread the program throughout Texas."

"I'm proud of you, son. You never gave up. I'm just so very proud."

Those words meant so much to Rey. He knew his father always loved him, but to make him proud for accomplishing something so close to his heart provided a special feeling on par to when Christina said yes and when Maddie and Noah were born.

Rey practically floated home. He thought about all the exciting things he would do with RIHARP, but his mind drifted to his number one priority: moving Christina and the kids back in. First, he needed to tell her the good news.

Once inside, Rey called David into the family room. "Could you sit down for a second? I have a big announcement to share with Christina and I want you to be here, too."

David tilted his head and sat down slowly. "Okay."

Rey hit send and after one ring Christina answered.

"So?" she prompted, anticipating news.

"Hi, hon. How's your day going?" Rey responded in a sullen voice.

"Oh no, I'm so sorry. I was hoping you were calling to report good news."

Rey couldn't continue with the ruse any longer. "I am. RIHARP was approved!"

David beamed and gave Rey a high-five.

Christina gasped, "For real?"

"Yes, and I got promoted to director of community relations. They want me to go out and grow RIHARP around the state."

"Wow, honey, that's awesome. Your dad is going to be so excited."

"I already told him."

"What did he say?" Christina asked.

"I heard him cry for the first time in my life."

CHAPTER FIFTY-ONE

Three days later, on move-in day for Christina and the kids, Rey finished taking the last load from his truck into his house. On his way to Noah's room, he noticed something in the family room that stopped him in his tracks. Christina and David sat next to each other on the couch. They looked up when they saw Rey gawking at them.

"We both love Judge Judy. Now I have someone who will watch with me." Christina looked at David and they both smiled at Rey.

Everyone grew more comfortable with the new living arrangement. Rey made breakfast for the kids every morning while Christina put the finishing touches on decorating all the rooms. She also interviewed several real estate agents to sell their San Antonio house.

Maddie and Noah learned that David like to draw comics and after he learned to construct G-rated versions, he shared them with the kids. They were his biggest fans and he reveled in their glee with each new comic story.

A week after Christina moved back into the Austin house, she walked into the kitchen where Rey was seated at the kitchen table. She stopped at the table and stared at a piece of mail.

"Something wrong?"

"This is for David." Christina handed Rey the envelope, which had a return address of the Huntsville prison in Houston.

Rey stared at the envelope. "I wonder what this is all about."

Christina gave the letter to David when he came into the kitchen for dinner. Rey and Christina watched David open the envelope and read the letter. They studied his expression carefully, hoping for some clues about the letter's content. When David finished reading the letter, he tossed it on the table and looked at Christina and Rey.

"I've got an interview with the lead voter of my parole board. "A half smile appeared on David's face.

"You're up for a parole?" Christina inquired.

"Yeah, I've served fifty percent of my sentence so I'm eligible to apply now. My eligibility date is in early April. I applied four or five months ago. After things started going better here, I asked for a live meeting. I thought that may help my case."

"That's great!" Christina said she snatched up the letter.

"Yeah, now I just need to share how much I changed since I've been here. The meeting is in three weeks."

Rey moved next to Christina and David as they looked down at the letter on the kitchen table. This single piece of paper provided David with more hope than anything else the previous two decades.

"We'll help you, David." Rey offered. "We will build the most compelling case for you that the Texas Parole Board has ever seen."

David turned toward Rey but wouldn't look him in the eye. Tears welled in his eyes and his lips were quivering. "You'd do that for me?"

Rey reached out and grabbed Christina's hand. She squeezed it back.

"Absolutely."

• • •

First, they focused on forgiveness. They shared the need to seek and extend forgiveness. By the beginning of the second week, David was ready to apologize and ask for forgiveness from the families of all three victims. It took a few more days, but after a long meeting with his counselor, David also agreed that he would try to forgive his father for a childhood of abuse.

"I didn't realize that forgiving someone could also make me feel better." David chimed in after the breakthrough moment.

Next, Christina and Rey had David write down everything he learned in prison that would help him make better decisions in the future. The initial list contained two items in his bulleted list, but Christina helped him identify a dozen more.

Last, Rey wanted David to develop a plan to stay on the right path after his release.

"How do you plan to handle another request from an old friend from Houston or a former inmate to help them or you by breaking the law again?" Rey asked David.

"I hope that never happens again." David replied.

"Hope isn't a strategy. Just like they teach everyone in the military, you need to have a plan so that when the bullets start flying you know what to do. You need to have a plan for anything that may cause you to stumble once you're released."

David nodded and got to work.

His plan contained examples of how he would handle temptation, frustration, anger, and financial constraints once released. David also noted several instances of his ability to make positive choices during his last few months with RIHARP.

During the last week, Christina and Rey role-played with David and asked the questions they suspected he might be asked during his interview.

The night before David's meeting with the lead voter, Rey closed his notes. "I think you're ready, David. Get a good night's sleep so that you are fresh tomorrow."

After dropping off the kids at school, Rey and Christina took David to the parole hearing in Huntsville. A parole officer guided David to his interview room while Rey and Christina found seats in the visitors waiting area. Christina sat with her knees bouncing and leaned over with her hands in a prayer position. Rey kept looking at his phone to check the time.

"Will he find out today?" Christina asked.

"No, it will take a couple of weeks to get a final decision from the board."

"So, I'm going to have anxiety like this for another two weeks?" Christina shrieked.

"I'm afraid so. It can take—"

David emerged from the interview room. The parole officer handed David back to Rey and Christina.

"How'd it go?" Christina asked.

"I don't know," David snapped. "I don't want to talk about it. She asked me a million questions over the last half hour, and I don't think I gave the right answers. I just want to get back to my room in Austin."

Christina and Rey exchanged concerned glances and honored his request. Few words were spoken during the three-hour drive back to Austin.

David withdrew from the Mendozas over the next two weeks. He spent more time in his room and was less talkative during dinner. He even stopped playing outside with Maddie, Noah, and Patches like the four of them did regularly before the parole hearing. Christina found herself watching Judge Judy alone most afternoons.

"I'm concerned about David. He seems like he's depressed," Christina shared with Rey when they were getting ready for bed.

"Yeah, maybe."

"I'm concerned he may hurt himself if they deny his parole. What do you think?"

Rey pursed his lips and exhaled. "I am concerned he won't get parole and if it happens, we'll have to keep a close eye on him."

"How could they not give him parole? He seems like a textbook case of redemption and he's ready to be a good citizen now."

"I agree, but I don't recall any inmates that got parole having to wait over two weeks. It seemed like they all knew within a week or so. I hope they aren't using RIHARP against him."

"How?"

"It's new for everyone, including the parole board, so maybe they think he hasn't served enough time behind bars. Some may also think he changed due to an unfair advantage."

"Now *that* would be unfair," Christina said.

"I just hope that all the good I see coming from RIHARP doesn't end up hurting David."

CHAPTER FIFTY-TWO

Work was a welcome distraction for Rey. The Project Second Chance team was preparing to publish the RIHARP manual and distribute it to all the TDCJ facilities in the next four weeks.

Annie stopped unexpectedly at Rey's desk. "Can you come with me to Deputy Director Scalise's office?"

Rey was quite familiar with the route to the deputy director's office, but he followed Annie. "Is something wrong?" he asked.

"You'll see when you get there."

Rey noticed a woman sitting in a chair across from the deputy director when he entered the office. She didn't look familiar. He stood next to the open chair next to her.

"Please, sit down," Mr. Scalise said while motioning to the empty cushioned chair.

Before Rey could sit, the woman stood up and extended her hand. "Hi, I'm Carla from the Huntsville parole board."

Rey swallowed hard. Did they send a person to deliver the bad news? Where they also worried that David might harm himself?

"Hi, Carla. I'm Rey Mendoza. It's a pleasure to meet you," Rey said with a fake smile he wasn't sure she believed.

Carla and Rey sat down and faced Deputy Director Scalise.

"Well, we have a pretty unique situation with David Kimbell," Carla shared. She turned to Rey. "Is Mr. Kimbell home now?"

"Yes, he is."

"Okay, I have some news that I want to share with Mr. Kimbell. I'll tell you two first and then I'd like to follow you home to tell him. Please don't call or tell anyone else before I can tell David in person."

Rey listened to her news and then went back to his desk to get his truck keys. He checked his mirrors every few seconds to make sure Carla was still behind him on the way to his house. Rey thought about calling Christina to warn her about the pending news, but he promised Carla that he wouldn't tell anyone and he intended to honor that promise. Plus, Rey wanted Carla to break the news to David.

Twenty minutes later, Rey unlocked the back door and entered the kitchen. Christina heard the deadbolt turn and scampered toward the door to verify it was Rey. Her expression warmed with a smile when she saw Rey, but it vanished when she noticed a middle-aged woman in a TDCJ corrections uniform behind him.

The concerned look on Christina's face was beamed to Rey. He darted over to help put her mind at ease. Rey knew is wife well, so he knew she was thinking bad news was on the horizon.

"Honey, this is Carla. She is from the Huntsville parole board. David interviewed with her a couple of weeks ago and she has some news to share with him."

"Did he get his parole?"

Rey turned to Carla. She smiled and replied, "I would like to share the news directly with David before I tell anybody else. You are free to come with us if you like."

Christina nodded.

Rey led the party of three to David's room. Rey knocked on the door and opened it after he heard David yell to come in.

David sat up and swung his legs over the side of the bed. His face turned pale when he saw a familiar face in a corrections uniform.

Rey spoke first. "Carla is here to share some news with you."

Christina's body stiffened as she stood next to Rey. Carla sat next to David.

"David Kimbell, I have a resolution on your request for parole."

The room was so quiet, Rey could hear the refrigerator hum in the kitchen. It seemed like minutes passed, but a second later Carla revealed the reason for her visit.

"The State of Texas is granting you parole."

David jumped up and pumped his fist. He leaned down to give Carla a hug then quickly reconsidered his actions.

"It's okay." Carla smiled.

David gave Carla a quick hug.

She continued, "This was the easiest decision I've made in my fourteen years on the parole board. You embraced your opportunity with the RIHARP program and made the most of it. I wanted to tell you the good news personally and tell your hosts that they did a great job preparing you for life outside of the corrections system. I hope I get to see a lot more cases like this in the future."

Christina hugged Rey. David noticed their embrace and started a group hug in the doorway of his bedroom.

Carla broke up the hug fest, saying, "I have one more bit of good news to share."

Everyone turned back to Carla sitting on the bed.

"It's effective immediately," she continued. "David Kimbell, you are officially on parole as of now."

The three embraced again. This time with tears comingling with smiles.

Carla stood and turned toward Rey and Christina.

"I need to brief David on his next steps. I'll share the conditions of his parole, reentry options and a visit to Sectronix to disarm Sure Cuffs. You're welcome to stay, but it's going to take a while."

Christina grabbed Rey by the hand and pulled him to the door.

"We're going to give you two some privacy to discuss his life as a free man."

The next day, Christina and Rey stood outside the bedroom door as David finished packing his belongings. David took one final look around the room and then he zipped up his new duffel bag, a parting gift from the Mendozas. He threw the long strap over his shoulder and moved toward the door to say his final goodbye to Rey and Christina.

"Where you heading?" Christina inquired.

"A taxi is on the way. They set me up with transitional housing for the next month, so I have time to find a job and a place to live. I can't wait to get going."

"I'm proud of you, David," Christina said. "I had my reservations at first, but now after getting to know you I couldn't be happier that you're a free man. Please stay in touch."

Christina opened her arms and David embraced her in a tight hug. Both were crying.

Rey shook David's hand. "You've come a long way, buddy. I want to keep in touch, but hopefully not through my employer."

David gave Rey a light punch in the arm. "You ain't ever going to see me on the other side of those concrete walls again."

CHAPTER FIFTY-THREE

A month after RIHARP approval and starting his new position, Rey scored his first meeting to pitch a partnership with RIHARP. He entered the dimly lit room and sat in the same seat he had the previous year. This time Rey purchased his own coffee and had one waiting for Pastor Scott.

When Pastor Scott arrived, they exchanged a quick hug and sat down.

"Good to see you," the jovial preacher blurted.

"You, too." Rey leaned forward. "I really appreciate the advice you gave me. My wife and kids are back home with me, and we couldn't be happier."

Pastor Scott extended his hand for a high-five. Rey caught the cue and smacked hands with the preacher.

"That's awesome, Rey. I'm so happy for you and your family."

"I appreciate it, but that's not everything. If you remember from our last meeting, I had an inmate living with me. Well, he turned his life around and gave his life to Christ on my front porch. He just got released on parole. The board said it was the easiest decision they've made in a decade."

Pastor Scott stared at Rey with his mouth open. "I don't know what to say. I'm speechless." He shook his head for a few more seconds. "What an amazing story. I wish more people in prison could get a second chance like that."

"That's why I'm here."

Pastor Scott's smile vanished, and a serious look formed on his face. "What do you mean?"

Rey explained the entire RIHARP program and how it was now open to Texas citizens to host their own inmate. "I plan to travel around the state to solicit support from the faith-based community to support RIHARP and I'd love for Hill Country Community Church to be first."

Pastor Scott put his elbow on the table and rested his chin in his hand. He stroked the non-existent hair on his chin. "I do like the mission and we have a very generous church. What do you need from me?"

Rey straightened up in his chair. "I only need fifteen minutes in front of your congregation. If you give me the time, I'll bet that by the end of the summer you'll have members of Hill Country Church hosting inmates to provide a second chance."

Pastor Scott turned his attention from a spot high on the wall to his phone. Rey waited patiently while he scrolled through several screens.

He stopped scrolling and looked deeply into Rey's eyes, then he tapped his lips with his index finger. "The current series ends the week after next, so I have an open sermon in three weeks. Will that work for you?"

Rey nodded with a wide smile. "Yes, it does."

Pastor Scott stood up and shook Rey's hand. "I look forward to seeing the changes this program can bring to our community."

Three weeks later, Pastor Scott introduced Rey to his congregation. Rey took the stage and shared the information on RIHARP. He observed most of the parishioners listening patiently to his presentation detailing his new program to serve the community. One woman near the front caught Rey's eye. She was hanging on to his every word.

Rey made a mental note of the lady and the man and young

woman next to her. He hoped they would be the first family to sign up for RIHARP.

The End

LAST SECOND CHANCE

A convicted murderer. A caring family. Under one roof.

Find out about the first family that signs up for RIHARP and the danger they face when their inmate arrives.

Read Last Second Chance - Book 2 in the Dangerous Redemption Christian Suspense Collection

---

Rick Powell's relentless dedication to succeed serves him well. He expects the same results when he gets sucked into the family business.

He's wrong.

Things implode, and the bank wants its money back. Generations of hard work look to be lost forever.

Out of options, Rick and his wife accept an inmate into their home to gain some quick cash....and provide a second chance.

At first, it appears to be a stroke of genius, but incarcerated felons are unpredictable. Nothing goes as planned.

Will granting an inmate a second chance be a deadly mistake?

CONNECT WITH ME

Join My New Release Text List

Text **NEW** to **(844) 465-7100** to receive a text notification of each new book I release. Nothing else. Ever.

You can also text me at **(844) 465-7100** to tell me what you liked, disliked or anything else you want to share. I love to hear from readers and personally respond to all texts.

If you want to receive more frequent updates about discounts and promotions, exclusive stories and new releases, sign up for my author email newsletter at:

https://robertgoluba.com/newsletter

ACKNOWLEDGMENTS

Thank you to Lauren Goluba. The toughest, yet most helpful beta reader I know. My stories are better because of you.